ELIZA PROKOPOVITS

Her Enchanted Tower

Copyright © 2023 by Eliza Prokopovits

All rights reserved. No part of this publication may be reproduced, stored or transmitted in any form or by any means, electronic, mechanical, photocopying, recording, scanning, or otherwise without written permission from the publisher. It is illegal to copy this book, post it to a website, or distribute it by any other means without permission.

This novel is entirely a work of fiction. The names, characters and incidents portrayed in it are the work of the author's imagination. Any resemblance to actual persons, living or dead, events or localities is entirely coincidental.

First edition

This book was professionally typeset on Reedsy. Find out more at reedsy.com

Contents

Acknowledgement	iv
Chapter 1	1
Chapter 2	9
Chapter 3	17
Chapter 4	25
Chapter 5	36
Chapter 6	45
Chapter 7	55
Chapter 8	65
Chapter 9	76
Chapter 10	82
Chapter 11	87
Chapter 12	98
Chapter 13	104
Chapter 14	114
Chapter 15	123
Chapter 16	134
Chapter 17	142
Chapter 18	149
Chapter 19	158
Chapter 20	167
Her Accidental Frog: Chapter 1	180
Also by Eliza Prokopovits	192
About the Author	193

Acknowledgement

Thank you to everyone who continues to make this publishing dream possible:

Thank you to God for saving me and sticking with me, no matter what.

Thank you to my family for their support and encouragement, for cheering me on and talking me down from the ledges, for reminding me to have faith when it's hard.

Thank you to Megan Records, my editor, and Karri Klawiter, my cover designer, for helping me make each book as pretty and polished as possible.

Thank you to Aly, who catches the errors I miss—you're the best <3

Thank you to the community of authors and reviewers for the support you give to all of us.

Thank you especially to my readers for nerding out with me in Regency England. I'm so grateful for you.

Chapter 1

Catherine Whitmer was bored. Not just today or because it was raining. Every day. Her life was stiflingly dull.

Mama repeatedly assured her that all young ladies of a certain class spent their days embroidering and painting and practicing their music. Mama always followed that with an arched brow and, "You're quite lucky, you know, Kitty. Many ladies have no access to the quantity of books you read."

Catherine didn't doubt that Mama was right about the books, but she couldn't help feeling that she was missing out on a great deal of life. Surely other young ladies had better things to fill their time with than histories and geographies or even novels. Not that Mama let Catherine read novels often, but sometimes as a special treat she'd bring one home from the lending library when she'd been to the market. Books of magic were nearly as good as novels—they were a good bit more useful than the biography of William the Conqueror that sat forgotten on Catherine's lap, at any rate.

Catherine sighed and leaned her elbow on the tiny, narrow windowsill, one finger holding her place in the book while her attention drifted. The gray sky she'd woken up to had let loose, and now a dull, steady rain fell. The drab, dreary world outside her window felt like too accurate a reflection of her life. No one would be out in this weather, and like so many times over the past six years, Catherine could easily pretend that she and Mama were the only two people in the world.

Eventually, the rain tapered off. A pale, weak sun shone faintly through the dissipating clouds. Catherine placed her bookmark and set the biography aside. She loved the way the garden looked after rain, and this would be the perfect time to try out her new watercolors. She gathered her papers, easel, paints, and a blanket to sit on before tying an apron over her morning dress. Wrapping a worn green shawl around her shoulders, she gathered everything else into her arms and descended the winding staircase that carried her through each open level of the tower. Mama, her humming blending with the whirring of her spinning wheel, didn't look up as Catherine passed through.

"I'm going outside to paint," Catherine called.

"Dry off the bench first," Mama advised, still not looking up.

Catherine wound down another three levels to the kitchen, where she wrangled the heavy wooden door open without dropping anything. She paused on the wooden steps outside to breathe. The air smelled so fresh and clean and full of life, and the brightening sun glittered on the water that dripped from every leaf and twig and gleamed on each flagstone. The garden was barely recognizable in such a magical light. It looked fae and enchanted and full of possibility. Catherine could forget, as she carried her supplies to the bench in the farther corner, that she'd spent hours weeding the vegetable beds just yesterday.

The bench was as wet as everything else, of course. Catherine carefully lay her easel and paint set on the ground to free up one hand, which she held open and flat over the bench. She

CHAPTER 1

murmured a spell-word and couldn't stifle the giggle that came when the warm air rushed from her hand to dry the stone surface. This spell tickled, and she could only do it for so long before she had to stop and itch her palm. It was enough, however, and she laid the folded blanket on the bench to sit on. In a moment, she had her easel set up with paper, paints, and brushes at the ready. She'd forgotten to bring out a cup of water, so she skipped back inside to get one, then looked around to choose a subject for her painting.

Her eyes fell on the tower. The rain had made the stones darker so that it looked almost sinister as it loomed over the sprawling garden. It was an old round tower from the time of the Norman invasion—hence her choice of biography, however tedious—with a few broken bits of wall jutting jaggedly from the base. There had been more to the old building, but it had been unsalvageable ruins when Mama had first moved in, and the crumbled walls now formed part of the boundary of the garden, which was an asymmetrical not-quite-square. Catherine had always found the tower to be a rather romantic home, especially when she was in a gothic mood after reading a good novel, and she wondered how many people were lucky enough to live in a stone ruin. It wasn't easy to reclaim or maintain a tower like this. One needed a good deal of either money or magic to make it livable. Mama used magic.

Catherine began painting, letting the tower fill one side of her paper while the lilac walk and vegetable beds spread over the rest of the page. Birdsong and rainwater dripping from the leaves of the trees beyond the garden formed the background music to her art, and Catherine began to sing along. Singing to fill the silent loneliness was something she'd been doing for years, and she absently made up a song about rain in May.

She was on the fifth nonsense verse when a sound from the trees startled her. Whirling around, she froze, her mouth still open but the song choked off. Standing in the shadows beneath the trees stood a man and a horse. The horse blew again, and Catherine recognized the sound that had alarmed her, but she couldn't tear her eyes from the man standing at the horse's head.

He was somewhere between tall and short, perhaps a few inches taller than she was, and he wore an olive coat over tan breeches and black riding boots. The fabric clung to him as though he'd been caught in the tail end of the downpour. His cheeks reddened as she stared at him. "Forgive me for startling you. Your singing... I could have listened all day."

"Oh," was all Catherine managed. Her face felt hot, and she didn't know what to do with her hands. She twisted them in her apron as she glanced around the garden.

"You enjoy painting?"

He spoke as if he were grasping for a subject of conversation. Perhaps he'd been taught to avoid uncomfortable silences and to fill them with pleasant chatter. He couldn't be as nervous as she was.

"I'm... I'm not supposed to talk to strangers." Catherine's eyes fell on the tower, and she was glad Mama's window faced the other direction. *Not supposed to talk to strangers.* What an understatement. This man was the first person aside from Mama that she'd seen in six years.

A smile pulled at the gentleman's mouth, and Catherine watched his unexceptional features turn into something wondrous, full of humor and friendliness. "That's easy enough to rectify," he said, removing his hat and bowing. "I am Lord Henry Stanton, at your service."

CHAPTER 1

Catherine found herself smiling in turn. She rose and curtsied as Mama had taught her. "Catherine Whitmer. It's a pleasure to make your acquaintance."

"The pleasure's all mine, Miss Whitmer."

Catherine cringed at the name. "Oh, no, that won't do," she blurted without thinking, causing his eyes to widen in surprise. "That makes me sound stuffy and old like Mama."

He grinned and ran a hand through his hair. It was a medium brown, as unremarkable as the rest of him, but Catherine liked the way it ruffled messily. "What shall I call you, then?"

She hesitated. It wasn't the thing for a stranger to call one by one's Christian name, however much one might want to like them already. But his countenance was so open and genuine, she couldn't help trusting him. "I've always wanted to be Kate. Mama calls me Kitty, but it's not the same at all."

"No, I suppose not," he agreed. "Kate it is, then, and you may call me Henry." As they'd talked, he and his horse had drawn nearer to the garden wall. He leaned his hip against it now and studied Catherine. "So, Kate, now that we're not strangers, tell me: do you enjoy painting?"

Catherine pressed her lips together to keep her smile in check. Why did her cheeks feel like they were glowing? Henry was not as handsome as the heroes in the novels she'd read. His nose was a bit too big, and his jaw wasn't chiseled, and his shoulders didn't strain against the seams of his coat. His eyes were a vague, muddy shade she couldn't label. But his face was pleasant, and his smile warm, and his eyes held a hint of laughter that drew her in.

"I do," she said. "I enjoy sketching with charcoal as well, but watercolor seemed more suited to the scenery."

"Indeed, water is quite the theme today." Henry chuckled. "I ventured out too soon, when what I'd thought was the shower ending was only a lull."

"You ought to go home and change before you catch cold."

"I really ought to," he agreed. "A damp coat isn't the most pleasant thing on a cool day."

"I should think not," Catherine agreed, though she wouldn't have minded him staying a bit longer. Talking to someone besides Mama was refreshing in a way she'd entirely forgotten.

He smiled at her again and bowed, replaced his hat, and swung himself into the saddle. "It was a pleasure meeting you, Kate."

"Yes," Catherine said softly as he turned his horse and rode back into the trees. She stared after him long after he was gone.

***

By the time Catherine had put away her paints and gone inside for dinner, she had a completed watercolor and had long since stopped blushing. Mama's dark eyes examined the artwork critically. They were pretty eyes, with lovely, long, dark lashes, only hidden behind thick spectacles. Mama's thin lips pursed as she pointed out a few places where Catherine's technique could improve. Catherine took the instruction meekly, as it was no more than she'd expected. Mama treated everything as an opportunity for improvement, refusing to settle for less than perfection in any regard. She dismissed Catherine to put away her art supplies, urging her to hurry back down to set the table for dinner.

In her room at the top of the tower, Catherine took a moment to tidy away everything she'd gotten out. Mama was fastidious about housekeeping as well, and with such a small living space,

CHAPTER 1

Catherine couldn't deny that it was nice to have everything in its place and out of the way. Before she rejoined Mama in the kitchen, she paused by her window, gazing out over the garden and trees to the distant hills that shaded purple in the sunset. She slowly untied her apron, letting her mind wander for a moment. Somewhere out there, there were people. People who went about their lives with no idea that Catherine existed. Except one. Somewhere out there was a specific person named Henry who called her Kate and liked hearing her sing.

Catherine wrenched her mind away from these musings. She couldn't let on to Mama that anything different had happened today. She hung the apron on its hook on the wall and hurried down the stairs. Mama sliced a loaf of bread as Catherine got out plates and cups. As she maneuvered through the small space, trading places with Mama in their familiar dance of meal preparation, she noticed again how short Mama was, a few inches shorter than Catherine. Mama's long, dark hair was twisted at the nape of her neck in a severe knot. Catherine wondered if a softer style would suit Mama better, perhaps make her cheekbones appear less rigid, her chin less sharp. But soft was not the first word Catherine would use to describe Mama. Precise and perfectionistic, yes, and loving, in her own strict way. Catherine never doubted that Mama cared more for her than for anything in the world. But there were old secrets that made Mama afraid, and whenever Catherine came too close to asking about them, she was sent straight to bed.

Mama set the last serving dish on the table and sat across from Catherine. "What are you thinking of, Kitty? You look miles away."

"Not miles," Catherine said lightly. "I was wondering if you would let me try a new hairstyle on you, on a day when you don't have errands in the village. And I was thinking about how I might paint you, if you were ever to sit for me."

Mama's smile was faint but present. "I haven't done my hair in any other way since I was your age and attending balls in town."

Catherine itched to ask why *she* wasn't allowed to go to town, or even to attend any local assemblies, if Mama had been taken about by *her* mother. But that was a certain way to be sent to bed without finishing dinner, and Catherine was hungry.

When dinner was over and the dishes washed and put away, Catherine retired to her room, ostensibly to read for a short while by rushlight before going to sleep. But she didn't bother with the light. She used a spell that lit a flame in her palm so that she could see to find her nightgown, but she extinguished it quickly and got dressed in the dark. She slid between the sheets and pulled the wool coverlet up to her chin. Now, alone in the dark, she allowed her mind to wander again. Instantly, the charming stranger was before her eyes, leaning against the garden wall as he called her Kate. Warmth filled her belly as she remembered how his face lit up when he smiled and how his hair fell messily after he'd run his fingers through it. She wondered what color his eyes actually were. She wondered if, wherever he was, he was thinking of her, and whether she'd ever see him again.

Chapter 2

Henry rode home slowly, his mind full of Miss Catherine Whitmer. Kate. He couldn't believe how many times he'd ridden out that way in the past, ignoring the old tower as just another picturesque ruin. Today he'd ridden closer to it than usual, on an errand of mercy for his mother, and on the way home he'd heard the most beautiful voice. Thinking back on what words he could recall, the song was utter nonsense, but it hadn't felt that way at the time. Not coming from that sweet, lilting, angelic voice. He hadn't lied to Kate: if she hadn't noticed him, he may well have listened to her all day.

But he was just as glad she'd turned, because then he'd seen that her voice wasn't the only exquisite thing about her. Her golden hair had tumbled in a long, thick braid over one shoulder, with curls escaping in a kind of wispy halo. Her eyes were the vibrant blue of cornflowers and so open and curious and bewitchingly innocent. The rising pink in her cheeks had captivated him, and he'd felt awkward and shy for the first time since he couldn't remember when. A duke's eldest son was never awkward. Even in uncomfortable situations, he was always in the right.

He managed to push Kate from his mind as he arrived home

and reported to his mother that the rector's wife and new baby were healthy and that they were suitably grateful for the hamper she'd had the kitchens put together.

The next day Henry spent the morning with his father and Rogers, the steward, going over some planned improvements to the mill and the second greenhouse. He loved this land and his duties to it, and his mind remained fully occupied with business for hours. But Rogers had other work to do, and his father never liked being cooped up in an office for long. The three parted ways, with Henry declining to go fishing with his father. Too much sitting in the boat, too much quiet time to think—he'd rather be moving. He went for a walk around the park instead, and when that wasn't activity enough, he walked to the village.

The nearer half of the village was all on Caulder-owned land, and from the time he'd left university, Henry had made it his practice to occasionally volunteer in their tenant businesses and learn what they did and what they needed from their landlord. He'd helped the chandler several times, though he wasn't particularly fond of the smell of the tallow used to make the candles. He'd fed horses at the livery and helped the laundress hang clean clothes to dry. His favorite by far was working with leather—by hand, the way it had been done for generations, not in one of the newer factories—and after several sessions of assisting, he had bought his own small set of leather working tools to continue the hobby at home. Today, though, he made his way to the smithy. None of the shop owners ever allowed him to do any work that was dangerous or menial or even especially dirty, but he hoped today he could convince the blacksmith to let him hammer something. He needed to work out his distraction over the blonde beauty.

CHAPTER 2

Hours later, he returned to Cauldercrest sweating, dirty, and satisfied, only to have his thoughts invaded again as he cleaned up for dinner. What was it about Kate that intrigued him so much?

He'd have to see her again to find out, but that was a risk he couldn't take. Pursuing Kate's acquaintance might raise her expectations, and it would likely put his heart in danger of becoming attached. If she could fill so many of his thoughts after a five-minute meeting, how much of his mind and heart would she take over if given more time?

He had to remember that his duty was to his family and the duchy. He owed it to them to make a good match, whenever he was ready to choose a wife, which wasn't quite yet. He was only four-and-twenty, after all. He had time. Kate's situation was too mysterious and unknown to be a wise choice, so he simply had to force her from his mind.

His restless distraction continued the following day. He worked on a tooled leather satchel he'd been making for his sister Mary's upcoming birthday, but shaping the soft leather still allowed him too much time to think. Eventually, he gave it up and packed away his tools, then took his pistols out for a bit of target practice. He didn't consider himself a Corinthian by any means, but he was a decent shot, and he could drive a team or sit a horse as well as anyone. He'd even had a lesson or two with Gentleman Jackson, though pugilism wasn't his preferred sport. Now, however, the focus required to load, aim, and safely fire the pistols grounded him. By the time he returned to the house, he could join his family with composure.

The following morning, Henry paced the breakfast room as he waited for his family to come down. His sister Hannah was first, and she instantly noted his mood. She joined him at the window and rested a hand on his arm to still his pacing.

"What is the matter?" she asked softly. "You're pacing like a caged tiger. You're *never* bored when we leave town."

"I'm not bored," Henry said. "It's nothing."

Hannah scoffed. "You're worse than I am, and *I'm* the one stuck here with just Mama and Mary, as the Wintons and Lewises have gone early to Brighton for the summer." She fixed him with a sharp hazel eye. "Do you have a sweetheart? Is there a clandestine correspondence that I ought to know about?"

Henry considered his sister, feeling heat rise in his neck. She was five years his junior, just barely nineteen, but she had wit and common sense and the ability to hold her tongue, which their youngest sister, Mary, manifestly lacked. He'd probably regret telling her about Kate, but perhaps Hannah could help him make sense of why the girl had stuck so firmly in his mind.

"Ride out with me this morning," he suggested. "We both could use the fresh air and exercise."

"And you'll tell me then?"

Henry shrugged.

Voices outside warned them that Mary was on her way, brightly wishing everyone she passed a good morning as she came. Hannah left his side, making her way to the sideboard to fill a plate. Mary burst through the door just then with a cheerful greeting for everyone. Henry had never understood how the fifteen-year-old could be so happy so early every morning, but she was, and he smiled in spite of himself.

Before sitting to breakfast himself, Henry requested that their horses be saddled for a morning ride. An hour later, he and Hannah were retracing his route through the park toward the village. He could see the stone tower looming over the trees in the distance, and his heart beat faster.

Hannah drew her horse alongside his. "Start talking," she insisted. "Am I to assume you'll insist on the *utmost* secrecy, and I'll not share it with Mama or Mary on pain of death?"

Henry chuckled at Hannah's imitation of Mary's dramatics. "You assume correctly," he said. "Mama mustn't hear a word."

"Oooh, so it is a sweetheart."

"No, she is not," Henry denied quickly.

Hannah pressed her lips together to hide her grin, but it still lit up her hazel eyes.

Henry sighed. "Her name is Kate, and I met her the other day on my way home from visiting the rector."

"And...?"

He shrugged. "I don't know. I can't seem to stop thinking about her, despite the fact that I know nothing of her."

"There's a way to fix that."

Henry had been hoping Hannah would have a solution. "What is it?"

"Get to know her better."

A sigh of disappointment whooshed out of Henry. Her solution wasn't a way to get Kate out of his head; it was a way to rectify his lack of knowledge. Not helpful.

Hannah must have seen his reluctance. "Tell me what you *do* know about her."

"She's very pretty, with a singing voice like an angel," Henry admitted. "She enjoys drawing and painting. She hates to be called Miss Whitmer, and she's not allowed to talk to strangers."

Hannah frowned at the last point, but her face quickly brightened. "Where does she live?"

"That's the odd thing—she lives in that old tower with her mother."

"The tower?" Hannah shot a look at the looming round tower on the far side of the village. "I thought it was a ruin. I didn't know anyone lived there."

"Neither did I, until I happened across Kate."

Hannah considered for half a moment then gave a decisive nod. "I want to meet her." She urged her horse into a trot.

Henry gaped at her for a moment before rushing to catch up. He'd known he'd regret telling her, but he'd merely expected her to tease him privately. He hadn't expected her to rush off and demand an introduction. He wanted to *avoid* seeing Kate again.

"Hannah, stop. You cannot just rush off like this. Why do you even want to meet her?"

"Because I could do with a new friend," she said, arching a brow at him. "All of mine have left the country for the summer. Just because you're not looking for a sweetheart doesn't mean *I* can't make her acquaintance."

She turned and rode on, leaving Henry to follow, a mixture of nerves and excitement twisting in his stomach. He did his best to squash the feeling—he didn't want to be happy at the prospect of seeing Kate again. But there was no denying that the feelings intensified as they left the shade of the trees and approached the garden where a blonde angel was bent over a trellis of pea vines, picking ripe pods.

She'd pinned her braid up today, and her morning dress was a pale yellow that made her appear to glow. At the sound of the horses, she looked up, surprise and delight flashing across her face at the sight of him, quickly chased by worry. She glanced over her shoulder at the tower, then abandoned her basket and hurried over to the low garden wall.

Henry watched her, entranced. He hadn't imagined or even

CHAPTER 2

exaggerated her beauty.

And then she was before them, her blue eyes sparkling. "I didn't think you'd come again."

"This is my sister, Lady Hannah Stanton," Henry said. "She insisted on an introduction as soon as I told her about you."

Beside him, Hannah curtsied, and Kate followed suit. "I'm delighted to meet you," Kate said, though there was an edge of tension that clung to her words. "And I'm sure I'm about to be terribly rude, but you need to leave now. Mama can't see you here, and she's bound to look out the window to check on me eventually."

"You're really not allowed to talk to strangers? I thought Henry was bamming me."

"No, not at all. And to Mama, *everyone* is a stranger."

"Is it just the two of you then?" Henry tried to make sense of the puzzle that stood before him. "If you're not allowed to talk to strangers—to *anyone*—then how do you make friends?"

Kate blinked at him. "You're the first new friend I've made in six years."

Her frank admission surprised him, especially in response to his relatively tactless question.

"Six years?" Hannah gasped. "Oh, you poor dear. I'm so glad Henry stumbled across you the other day and that we can be your friends now. We'll leave—I'd hate to get you into trouble—but could we come again?"

Kate nodded slowly. "Mama goes to the village on Monday and Thursday mornings. I'll hang something bright in my window—the very top one—to let you know that she's out and that it's safe to call up to me, and I'll come out to meet you."

"Brilliant," Hannah said, reaching for Kate's hand and squeezing it. "We'll come back soon."

Henry tipped his hat and helped his sister into the saddle. He couldn't help looking back over his shoulder as they rode into the trees. Kate was watching them as she backed slowly along the path toward the plants she'd been tending. She lifted her hand in a shy wave.

He faced forward again as Hannah said, "That poor girl needs a new friend even more than I do. I thought it was bad to have no one but the family for weeks, but six *years*?" She shook her head. "You're calling with me again on Monday."

Henry murmured an agreement. There was something odd about Kate's situation, and he was glad that Hannah had strong-armed him into seeing her again. Kate needed someone like Hannah to bring fresh life to her days, and Henry would be eaten alive by curiosity until he'd figured her out.

Chapter 3

Catherine fell asleep thinking of Henry and Hannah that night. They looked so much like siblings, and they seemed so natural that way. Hannah's smile was so like her brother's, and her hair, what Catherine had seen of it around Hannah's bonnet, was the same shade of brown. Her eyes were a clear hazel, not the muddy shade between brown and green that Catherine was fairly certain Henry's were. The top of her head only came up to her brother's chin, but they were unmistakeably not only related but close friends.

Seeing them had sparked a small flare of jealousy inside Catherine. How often had she longed for a large family? For siblings to play with? For anyone else to understand what it was like to live with Mama and her rules and her critiques?

The Stanton siblings had also inspired a deep longing to be around them more, to watch them together, to experience family vicariously. It was nonsensical, she told herself, and Catherine probably ought to be more wary of strangers as Mama had warned her. She knew she was naïve and sheltered. She'd been too little exposed to society to know what people were capable of. But she couldn't help trusting Henry and Hannah. They had such open, friendly faces, as if making acquaintances of strangers were a common occurrence for them. Perhaps it was. She knew nothing about them or their lives.

But she wanted to.

The weekend was cool and wet. Catherine hurried through her chores in the garden with her shawl hugged tight around her, then spent the rest of the days in her room or Mama's. She played the harp and sang, and while Mama had as many suggestions for improvement as usual, Catherine saw the way her body relaxed into the music and her eyes closed as she listened. Catherine's technique may not yet be perfect, but she still brought pleasure to her listener. After dinner, Mama read aloud while Catherine knit. It was a pleasant time, and peaceful, and for a few hours Catherine forgot about being Kate and wishing for a big family.

On Monday morning, Mama gathered her things and left for the village. Catherine, watching from her window, saw Mama cross the garden and pause to rest her hand on the wall before striding into the trees. Once she was out of sight, Catherine took out her brightest shawl, a delicate sky blue lambswool, and hung it over the windowsill, weighing it down with books so that it wouldn't fly away. Her heart fluttered for a moment like the shawl as it caught the light breeze. It was too much to hope that the Stantons would come again so soon, wasn't it? Catherine scolded herself for being silly and busied herself with her pencil and sketchbook, as she had no hope of concentrating on a book. She found her mind wandering as she drew, however, and her page filled with vague horse shapes. Horses had fascinated her as a child. She wondered if she might take the chance to draw Henry's horse some day when he visited. But that would risk Mama finding out—where would Catherine have come across a horse between the tower

CHAPTER 3

and garden to draw an accurate picture of one? No, she would have to content herself with vague sketches from memory.

But that didn't feel like enough. She sighed and closed the sketchbook, moving to the harp. She played softly, dreamily, enjoying the music for its own sake, not for its execution or performance value. Midmorning sun streamed through her narrow window, creating a puddle of light at her feet. Smiling at the idea of liquid sunlight, Catherine began to sing.

She didn't know how long she'd been singing when a familiar voice hailed her from down in the garden. Her heart sped up as her fingers faltered on the strings. She rushed to the window, and there he was, grinning up at her, with a beaming Hannah by his side. Henry waved, and she returned it before scooping up the shawl from the window ledge. She wrapped it around herself as she hurried down the stairs and out the door.

They were tying their horses to a branch of the nearest tree where they could graze as they waited.

"Your horse is beautiful," Catherine said, resting her hands on the wall, sensing the spell Mama had left there. "What's its name?"

Henry looked up at her, patting the chestnut horse's neck. "This? This is Honey." He blushed at Hannah's snort of laughter and rubbed the back of his neck. "Officially, his name is Mercury because he's so fast, but when I bought him, Mary called him Honey, and the name stuck. Would you like to meet him?"

Absolutely, yes, but Catherine shook her head. "I can't leave the garden. Will you come in and walk with me? And tell me about Mary?" She gestured back to the flagstone paths behind her.

Hannah was beside her in a moment, with Henry close

behind. "You're not allowed to leave the garden?"

Catherine shook her head, breathing a silent sigh of relief that they passed the wall. She'd held a secret fear that Mama had a spell to keep strangers out. "It's the second cardinal rule of my life. Mama even put a spell on the garden wall so that I can't pass through." She shot a glance at Henry. "For my protection, of course." Mama's excuse came easily to her lips, but that didn't mean she believed it. She turned and began walking along the garden path with Hannah to one side and Henry on the other.

He stared at her. "Your life must be *stifling*."

Catherine smiled ruefully. She'd had that very thought herself. "At times."

"I couldn't have borne it," Hannah said. "I'd have run away."

"Oh, I've tried," Catherine said. "Twice. Once, when I was thirteen, I snuck out in the middle of the night, and then when I was fifteen I left while she was in the village. That's when she started enforcing the boundaries with magic."

It surprised her that Mama hadn't cast a broader spell to keep strangers out, as well as to keep her in, but she supposed such a one didn't exist. Mama must need a very particular person in mind to cast the barrier spell. She didn't want to think what would happen if Mama ever found out about Hannah and Henry.

She paused and looked up at each of them. They were close enough now that she could see a light dusting of matching freckles across each of their noses and cheeks. "I didn't get far either time I tried, and, really, where would I go? I know no one. I have no other family. And for all her overprotectiveness, I know she loves me."

Henry's eyes were so solemn and full of compassion that she

couldn't hold his gaze. She began walking again and turned to Hannah.

"Tell me about your family," she said. "Who's Mary?"

"Our youngest sister," Hannah said.

"How many of you are there?"

"Four," Henry said. "We also have a brother, Daniel, who is between us in age. He's one-and-twenty, and he's just finishing at Oxford. He'll be a clergyman."

"And then you're…" She looked at Hannah.

"Nineteen. I've just had my first Season in town. And Mary's fifteen."

"I've read about the London Season," Catherine said, remembering the few novels Mama had brought home. "Did you find a beau? Isn't that what the Season is for?"

She heard poorly stifled laughter from Henry, and Hannah's eyes went wide. Catherine blushed.

"I'm so sorry—I've said something wrong, haven't I? I'm both ignorant and dreadfully curious."

Hannah chuckled and took Catherine's arm, looping it through hers. "You're refreshing," she said. "Don't change a bit. And, yes, Mama was trying to arrange a match for me, but no, nothing came of it. I'm in no hurry."

"Unlike Mary." Henry's lips curved in an amused smirk, his expression soft as he mentioned their youngest sister.

"Unlike Mary," Hannah agreed. "She's all too eager for her first Season, and she's determined that she'll fall in love at first sight and be married by June."

"With her temperament, she'll do just that," Henry added, "though I hope she'll choose well when the time comes."

"Do you believe in love at first sight?" Catherine asked. "It's very common in books, but I don't know how likely it is in reality. What do you think?"

Hannah's cheeks tinged slightly pink. "I don't think it's impossible," she said.

"But it's not common, or at least not for that instant attachment to be the start of something real," Henry put in. "Regardless of when and how the feelings begin, I'd prefer to take the time to get to know the woman I marry."

"Time spent getting to know someone, let alone falling in love," Catherine said, smiling up at him. "To me it almost sounds too good to be true. But I suppose to anyone else it wouldn't seem quite as wonderful."

"I'd imagine that it's always wonderful to spend time with the object of one's affection."

Hannah hummed her agreement, and they walked in silence for a moment. Catherine wanted to ask a dozen more questions, but she didn't want to sound ignorant or impertinent again. Henry was the one to break the silence.

"What would you do first if you could leave the garden?"

Catherine had been watching the horses grazing at the far end of the garden, and she didn't need to think about her answer. "Beg you to let me ride Honey."

Henry laughed. "Can you ride?"

Catherine shook her head. "No. I suppose I'd have to ask you to teach me."

"It would be my pleasure. What else would you do?"

"I'd go to a ball." She shot sidelong glances at both siblings. The revelation didn't seem to surprise Henry, given that he had two sisters and must be used to such wishes. "To get all dressed up and dance with actual people to actual music..."

"Do you dance, then?" Hannah asked, her expression bright.

Catherine nodded. "Mama gives me dance lessons every

winter, when it's too cold or wet to take exercise outside. But with only two of us, we must either dance together to the sound of our unaccompanied singing or Mama plays the harp while I practice alone." She watched the breeze make a nearby lilac blossom dance and sway, adding, "I like dancing, but I'm convinced that I'm missing out on the full enjoyment of it."

"You are," Hannah agreed. "We shall have to find a way to get you to a ball."

Catherine laughed. Her new friend's kindness was sweet, but she couldn't forget that this entire conversation was hypothetical. To prove the point, as the path led along the outer wall, she stepped apart from the others and reached out a hand, pushing against the air above the wall. It seemed like perfectly ordinary air until she leaned beyond the wall, and then it thickened until it was like trying to move through molasses. Catherine caught Hannah's eye, raised a brow, and then straightened. "We would have to find a way past the boundary spell first," she said.

"Do you know what spell she uses?" Henry asked.

She shook her head. "She casts most of her spells without speaking, and I've never come across this one in any of the spell books I've read."

Henry looked thoughtful, and they made another loop of the garden without speaking. Catherine was used to quiet, and somehow silence with Henry and his sister was perfectly comfortable. Just having them nearby made the day seem brighter and the garden more inviting.

"Forgive us, Kate," Henry said. "We should have thought to ask: how long is your mother usually in the village?"

Catherine looked at the position of the sun. "Goodness, I've lost track of time. She'll be back within a half hour." Her stomach fluttered with sick nerves at the thought of Mama returning and finding the Stantons there.

"I wish we could stay," Hannah said. "There are so many more things for us to talk about. We haven't even mentioned drawing or music. You said she goes out again on Thursday? May we visit again?"

It warmed Catherine's heart that they wanted to see her again. "I'll hang my shawl in the window."

Hannah grinned and squeezed Catherine's arm before releasing it. Henry took her hand and pressed it between his. Then the two mounted and rode into the trees.

Catherine wandered to the nearest bench and sank onto it. Emotions swirled within her as she relived every moment of their visit. She was certain that Hannah would be a dear friend, and the way Henry had grasped her hand in farewell set her stomach fluttering in a way she'd never felt before.

Chapter 4

On Thursday, Catherine was sitting at her window with charcoal and paper, sketching her sweeping view of the surrounding countryside, so she heard and saw the two horses leave the small, sparse forest that separated the tower from the road. Henry's face immediately turned up toward her window, and she waved. He waved back before saying something to Hannah. Catherine wasted no time setting aside her drawing supplies and racing down the stairs. She slowed when she passed through the outer door, however. The two Stantons had dismounted and were just entering the garden.

"Thank you for coming," she said, as Henry bowed and Hannah took her hands and squeezed them.

"I've been dying to talk to you again since we left," Hannah said, looping her arm through Catherine's. "We hardly had any time to get to know each other last time. You dance and you paint, and Henry says you sing like an angel, but I want to know more."

Catherine darted her eyes at Henry, who pretended not to hear, though his ears looked a bit red. He followed along behind them as they walked, Hannah asking questions and Catherine answering them as quickly as they came. They soon established that they both loved music, and that Bach was their favorite composer to play, though Hannah preferred to listen to Vivaldi's violin concertos.

When Catherine admitted that she'd never heard them, Hannah said, "We'll have to take you to a concert in town someday," as if it were the easiest thing in the world.

Catherine looked at Henry again in confusion, wondering if she ought to remind his sister that there was a spell limiting her to the garden. He merely smiled at her, and she reflexively smiled back.

Both girls enjoyed drawing and had read several of the same books. Both could speak French and Italian, though with varying fluency. By the time Henry and Hannah took their leave, it seemed to Catherine that they'd covered every topic and had agreed on nearly everything.

***

That evening, Catherine sat in the library, the room just below her own in the tower. Shelves of books lined the lower half of the wall from the staircase to the opposite window. A small hearth occupied the center of the other half of the curved wall, and Catherine's worn brocade chair was pulled near it. The day had been warm, but evening had brought a chill breeze, and the tower was drafty. Mama sat in the matching chair beside her, humming quietly to herself as she darned a pair of stockings. Catherine held a book open in her lap, a novel Mama had brought home from her trip to the village the day before.

Unbidden, Catherine's mind wandered back to the Stantons' visit during her mother's absence. Hannah had mentioned

CHAPTER 4

taking Catherine to town to see a Vivaldi concert, and though she knew it was impossible, she couldn't help but wish to go. It was frustrating, that things that were so commonplace and easy to Hannah and Henry were unattainable dreams to her.

"Where is your mind wandering off to, Kitty?" Mama asked, snipping off the end of yarn with her tiny shears. "Did you forget that you were reading?"

"I suppose I did." Catherine tried to laugh off her own absence of mind. She looked down at the book, where her finger marked the spot.

It was by a Miss Austen, and Catherine both loved the story and wished she'd never begun reading it. It had none of the absurdly dramatic flair of the Gothic novels Mama had brought home, which were laughably unrealistic even in Catherine's sheltered opinion. No, this story felt much closer to ordinary life, like the characters could live in a house down the road and Catherine could be friends with them if only she could leave the garden. To many readers, the events of the story might have seemed mundane, but in Catherine they set off a wave of longing. A country assembly where neighbors danced together. Morning calls from one's aunts and friends. A sister confessing her secret admiration for the gentleman next door. They were all things that she'd never experienced, and her heart ached at the lack.

Instead of beginning to read again, she asked, "Mama, why may we never go anywhere? Balls and parties must be lovely, but couldn't I even go to the village with you?"

"Hush, Kitty, we've discussed this. It isn't safe for you to go out. I can't lose you."

"But surely you could never lose me. Other people go out and about every day, and nothing terrible happens to them."

"You have no idea of the risks. You weren't there—you didn't hear…" Mama caught herself, and Catherine was sure she'd been about to let slip something secret and important.

"I wasn't there *when*?" Catherine asked. She opened her mouth to add, "What didn't I hear?" But Mama interrupted.

"That's enough novel reading for today. Silly, frivolous things that don't benefit your mind a jot. Go upstairs and practice the new piece I brought you, Kitty."

And the moment was over. There would be no secrets wrested from Mama tonight. Catherine marked the page and left the book on her seat, slowly climbing the stairs to her room to sit at her harp. Her mind was reeling with too many questions to focus on the new sheet music, so she warmed up with a familiar tune first, allowing the music to calm her and center her.

***

As Henry had feared, seeing more of Kate had led to thinking more of her. Her situation was so peculiar, locked away from the world with only her mother for company. He enjoyed her unaffected, forthright manner, which could only have come from such seclusion, but he couldn't help but think that such a charming girl deserved to see and be seen.

On Saturday morning, he found the house in a greater bustle than usual. Hannah, perceiving his perplexed frown, sat next to him at breakfast.

"You know Daniel arrives home today, don't you?"

Henry closed his eyes, stifling any sound that would make it obvious to the rest of the family that he'd forgotten. His head had been so full of Kate that he'd lost track of the date.

CHAPTER 4

"I do know," he murmured to Hannah, opening his eyes and returning to his plate. "But thank you for reminding me."

"Can I guess what you've been thinking of instead?" his sister teased softly. "Or *whom?*"

His sister knew him too well. "Don't be absurd," he said. "I am no more to her than you are."

Hannah smirked. "But I never said who I would have guessed."

Henry's ears grew hot, but he retorted, "Your suggestion was not subtle."

"Come on, Henry, it's obvious you admire her."

"Who wouldn't? But I'll thank you to stop trying to make a match for me. We wouldn't suit."

Hannah made a face as though he were a fool for spewing a blatant falsehood. "Very well, but you shan't get out of accompanying me. She's still *my* friend."

"I never said she wasn't my friend. I merely pointed out that I don't intend for her to become more."

"But why not?"

Henry ignored Hannah's demand and excused himself from the table as his mother and Mary came in. The last thing he needed was two more women picking up on Hannah's badgering and joining in. Mary would be even less circumspect in her teasing, and Mama would probably pay a call on Kate's mother. Henry would have to endure mocking and discomfort, but if Kate's mother found out about them—it would be misery for her.

If circumstances were different, Henry might have been interested in pursuing a relationship with Kate. She was sweet and bright and undeniably herself, and he enjoyed calling on her with Hannah a great deal. But there was too much mystery surrounding her. It would be irresponsible of him to marry a woman clouded by such unknowns. He could be her friend, like Hannah, but he really needed to rein in any thoughts that would lead to wanting more.

Henry got out his leather working kit to distract himself while the rest of the family finished breakfast, then they all prepared to welcome his brother home. Daniel had finished at Oxford and would be home for a month before taking his new position as rector of their uncle's parish. It was strange to think of Daniel making sermons, when Henry remembered the scrapes the two of them had gotten into together as children. But Daniel was steady and grounded, and he would set a good example for his parishioners. Henry had never had an inclination to join the church, but he hadn't needed one—he was to inherit his father's title and duties, and he hoped to set an equally good example as the next duke.

They welcomed the new graduate in the drawing room with hugs and kisses and demands, from Mother and Mary, that he tell them all of his news.

Daniel laughed. "I'm afraid I haven't much news. Nothing but studying and exams for me lately. But you've all been in town. Tell me about Hannah's introduction to the *ton*." He sat back and crossed one ankle over the other knee.

Henry unconsciously mimicked him. His brother had fairer hair and gray eyes, but otherwise they looked very much alike. They both listened quietly to the enthusiasm of their female relations, though Henry listened less attentively. He'd been present for all the events they mentioned, and his mind wandered to Kate and her wish to go to a ball. She'd love Almack's, though she'd surely find such a crush at the height of the Season overwhelming.

CHAPTER 4

"All in all, Hannah's debut was a great success," Mother concluded. "Now our next object is finding Henry a wife."

Henry straightened abruptly, his crossed foot coming to rest on the floor with a thump. His whole family was watching him. "I beg your pardon?" he spluttered.

Daniel grinned. "Should have known it was coming, brother. Hannah's come out could only buy you so much time."

"But she hasn't made a match yet."

"I will when I'm ready," Hannah said. "I'm in no rush."

"Neither am I. I have plenty of time."

"Not if you want a large family to succeed you," Father said, smiling proudly around at his four children. "You'll run the estates well, I've no doubt, but there's no harm in settling the line of inheritance early."

"And I want grandchildren," Mother added.

Henry gaped at them all. Hannah was biting her lip to keep from grinning as wide as Daniel. He took a deep breath. "I appreciate your concern, but I would beg you to give me leave to find the right woman in my own time."

"Oh, Henry, dear, I didn't mean you must marry next week." Mother waved her hand dismissively. "I meant only that I'll be looking for matches for you next Season with as much alacrity as for your sister."

Biting back a sigh, Henry nodded. As his brother had said, he ought to have expected this. It just seemed like his whole family was joining the matchmaking efforts today.

It was nice to have Daniel at home. The two brothers hadn't been in the same place much since Henry had left Oxford and the two had no longer been in school together. They spent a rainy Sunday afternoon playing billiards, which Henry consistently won, and cards, which he invariably lost.

"You're a terrible liar, Henry," Daniel said, shuffling the deck after trouncing him yet again. "That's why you're so bad at cards. I can always guess what cards you're holding."

"Does this mean you're a better liar? Because that's not something for a clergyman to boast of."

"I'm better at keeping my countenance impassive," Daniel said. "You're also not the best at reading the nuances of others' expressions. You're so open and straightforward that you want everyone else to be too."

Henry frowned. Kate was better off without siblings; their perceptiveness could be most unwelcome. Daniel wasn't wholly wrong. Henry could read people well enough if he tried, but sifting through the insincerities of the *ton* was an endless and exhausting task. Not that it took much work to see that every woman who sought his attention during the last Season had been interested solely in his title and wealth. That's why Kate's unaffected candor was so endearing.

But he couldn't go thinking of Kate again. He wrenched his mind back to the games at hand and to losing, yet again, to his brother.

Monday dawned bright and fair, and Mother informed the family at breakfast that they would leave right after breakfast for a picnic. Picnics were a regular occurrence in the summer at Cauldercrest, particularly when all the family were in residence. The ancient, shady willow by the lake where these picnics were always held was one of Henry's favorite spots in the estate and, by extension, in the world.

But for the first time, the thought of a family picnic made his heart sink. He and Hannah had intended to visit Kate today. She'd be expecting them, hanging her shawl in the window to signal that her mother was out. He exchanged looks with

CHAPTER 4

Hannah, but she subtly shook her head. She pulled him aside as they left the breakfast room.

"Are you prepared to tell Mama about Kate?" she whispered. "Because there's no way we're getting out of this without a full confession. Daniel's home, and picnics are a whole family event. Excusing ourselves just to go riding won't be enough."

Henry knew she was right. Confessing the truth to Mother would unleash chaos of epic proportions.

It was better to miss one visit.

The family gathered in the drawing room once everyone had changed for the excursion. Family picnics weren't formal by any means, but he couldn't help but note that his sisters and his mother all wore short kid gloves and decorative bonnets. As the weekend's rain had left the air a bit cool, they all wore long-sleeved walking dresses. They wore some variant on this every time they went out, and Henry had never paid attention before. Now it brought to his notice that Kate never wore a bonnet or gloves. Not that she'd need them in her own garden, particularly if she didn't expect to see another person, but there was something so very… innocent and uninfluenced by society about it.

He walked silently with the family along the lakeside path, listening to the idle banter between Daniel and their two sisters. It was a long walk, but they always chose to go on foot rather than horseback. By the time they reached the willow, which drooped to form a shady tent just up the bank from the lake shore, they were thirsty and beginning to be hungry again. While the servants laid out blankets and salads and lemonade, the girls picked wildflowers. Henry joined his father and brother for a game of cricket. He was distracted, however, by noting the progress of the sun across the sky—Kate's mother must have left by now—and his inattention earned him a solid thump from the ball as it hit his shoulder.

"Wake up!" Daniel called. He'd hit the ball that Henry had failed to catch. "Perhaps you'd do better picking wildflowers with Mary. You and Hannah can trade places."

Henry glared at his brother and tossed the ball back to his father so that he wouldn't whip it at Daniel. It was his own fault he'd gotten hit and made fun of, but that didn't improve matters. He did try to focus for the rest of the game, and he didn't hesitate to point out, when the game had ended and they made their way back to the blankets, that if they'd been keeping score, Daniel would have lost.

It was a beautiful afternoon. The food was good, and the breeze off the lake rustled the willow leaves and made a kind of soothing music. Henry's family talked and laughed. He loved his family, and he was grateful for this tradition. It was one he looked forward to continuing with his own children whenever he had them. Kate would probably love it too, he thought, before pushing her yet again from his mind. He stifled a frustrated sigh. The day would have been perfect if it hadn't been for the tugging in his belly, like a hook behind his navel, pulling him toward the girl in the tower. He shouldn't be having feelings like this for a mere acquaintance that he'd met less than two weeks ago.

As the sun sank lower and the family stood and prepared to walk back to the house, Henry suppressed the swell of disappointment at missing today's visit. He considered telling Hannah that he couldn't go with her on Thursday. He needed to distance himself from Kate if his emotions were going to get so tangled up over her. But he knew that would never happen—even if he could bring himself to say the words,

CHAPTER 4

Hannah wouldn't accept it.

Chapter 5

Thursday saw Henry mounted and riding with Hannah toward the tower. The more time passed since their last visit, the more that invisible connection tugged him toward Kate, and he hadn't resisted Hannah's insistence. To his chagrin, his heart sped up as he approached the tower and saw the shawl hanging from the highest window. Faint strains of music floated from above. It was lucky that he couldn't hear Kate's voice clearly from here; the sound would have held him spellbound, and Hannah would have gained even more ammunition to use in her matchmaking schemes.

The music stopped abruptly after his shout. They had just tethered the horses when the heavy wooden door swung open, and Kate barreled out. Her face lit up when she saw them, and Henry's heart softened.

She lifted her skirts and half ran, half skipped over to the wall. "You came!" She beamed, holding her hands out to Hannah. "I missed you."

Hannah took one of Kate's hands and left the other for Henry. He still wore his riding gloves, but Kate's hands were bare. Impulsively, he lifted her hand and brushed his lips over the soft skin of her knuckles. She flushed, and he suddenly wished he could kiss those rosy cheeks too.

CHAPTER 5

"I'm sorry we couldn't come on Monday," Hannah said. "Daniel's home, you see, and there were family plans that we couldn't get out of."

"Oh, shouldn't you be there with him, then?"

"He'll be here for a few more weeks. We'll have plenty of time." Hannah released Kate's hand and stepped into the garden, and Henry reluctantly did the same. Kate's warm fingers in his had pushed aside every logical argument he'd made against getting attached, and he didn't want to let go.

Kate smiled up at him before she turned and linked arms with Hannah. They began walking along the path, and Henry fell into step beside them.

"I won't pretend that I wouldn't be sadly disappointed if you never came back, but I know you have a life as well, however much I enjoy your company."

"We enjoy your company too, Kate," Hannah said. "Don't we, Henry?"

"Of course."

Her brilliant smile made his breath catch and his thoughts stutter to a halt. He was glad Hannah was there to carry on the conversation, because he couldn't form a coherent question.

"How did you spend your morning when we weren't here?"

"The same as usual," Kate said airily. "I read for a while and practiced the harp, then came outside to draw."

"What were you reading?"

"A book about William the Conqueror. I can't help but feel that history must have been very interesting, but history books are so dull I can hardly bear to read them. It's taken me weeks to finish this one."

She glanced up at him and blushed. Henry wondered if she expected him to deplore her lack of studiousness or if she, too, had been wrestling with a distracted mind recently.

"I couldn't agree more. Give me a book about nature any day," Hannah said. "I'd much rather read about animals and plants than old, dead kings. Though I suppose the Norman Invasion was interesting enough."

For a few minutes they talked about history. The tower that loomed over them had, apparently, been built during the Norman Invasion, which was why Kate had chosen the book to begin with. Though Henry was no stranger to history or to literary discussion, he couldn't remember ever enjoying such a conversation more.

At length, Kate said, "But what about you? Will you tell me about your family plans that kept you away? I don't mean to pry, and you needn't tell me if you don't wish to, but I confess I'm curious about family engagements, as I've had none."

For the millionth time, Henry wondered what had happened to cut her and her mother off from the world so completely. He told her about Daniel coming home and about their tradition of having picnics every summer.

"Mother insists on having at least one picnic when the whole family is at home, preferably more," he said.

Kate listened avidly as Hannah described the picnic spot under the willow. She told about collecting wildflowers while the men played cricket and how the lake glittered blindingly in the sun.

"We often end the day with headaches from the sun on the water, but no one seems to mind enough to stop going."

Kate smiled between the two of them. "Home and family are very important to you, aren't they?"

"They are," Henry agreed. "Both of our parents always made time together a priority, and they instilled that in us." When

CHAPTER 5

her smile turned wistful, he added, "Home and family are important to you too, judging by how eager you are to hear about ours."

She laughed softly. "Yes, I value them a great deal because I don't have them." She wrinkled her nose adorably and said, "This is my home, and at times I love it, but more and more it feels like a cage. And I love Mama, but she keeps secrets from me, and that's not what I think a family should be." She sighed.

"Secrets?" Hannah asked.

Kate shrugged. "There's so much she won't talk about. And isn't keeping me away from society just a way of keeping the whole world a secret?"

"I suppose."

She sighed and looked up at him, her vivid blue eyes earnest. "I crave freedom. Sometimes I almost wish that you had never come that first day, because then I wouldn't know what I was missing. I *don't* wish it—truly, I don't, because I treasure your friendship—" She rested her free hand on Hannah's forearm still linked through hers. "But you've given me a tiny taste of freedom, and now I crave it more and more each day."

Her intensity and heartbreaking honesty were captivating. If Henry weren't careful, he could lose himself in those flashing eyes. He found himself wishing that he could give her the freedom she desired, wishing to give her the world and the ability to explore it.

***

Daniel found Henry pacing the library that evening after dinner.

"You're not going to sit with the others? Mother said you

often read to them."

Henry shook his head. "Not tonight. I can't sit still."

His brother sat in a wing-backed chair by the door and watched him silently for a moment. "Want to tell me about her?"

Henry froze mid-step for a heartbeat, then continued his pacing. Of course his brother saw through him. He always did. "Not particularly."

"You've got to talk to someone," Daniel reasoned.

Henry had already talked to Hannah on the ride back from the tower. They'd agreed that something must be done, but neither could decide on what. Perhaps talking through the problem with an impartial party would straighten out his thoughts.

"Her name is Kate," he sighed. Before he could figure out what to say next, his brother interrupted.

"You're calling each other by your Christian names already?"

"It's not like that. She's a friend of Hannah's. She hates being called Miss Whitmer."

"How very singular."

"She is," Henry agreed. "In most respects." He came to a stop by the mantle and rested his arm on it. "Do we know any magicians?"

Daniel blinked at him, obviously startled by the non sequitur. "What for?"

"Kate has a magical dilemma, and I'd hoped to help her find the solution."

Asking a practicing magician was the one solution Henry had come to. He had little knowledge of magic, and the library, which Henry had searched before pacing, had a scant selection of spell books.

CHAPTER 5

Daniel steepled his fingers and pressed the point against his lips as he thought. "What about Harborough?"

Henry frowned. "I've never met him." The Duke of Harborough was several years older than Henry and had been in possession of the title for a while now. Henry vaguely remembered that their fathers had been friends, but he knew little more of the man.

"I had a few friends in the magic school at Oxford," Daniel explained. "Harborough graduated years ago, but they still talked about him as some kind of legend."

Henry's own acquaintances at university had been primarily in the fields of law or business, but Daniel had always had a gift for making friends with anyone.

He nodded slowly. "I'll write to him. Immediately." He moved toward the desk in the corner of the library as Daniel rose from his chair. "Tell Mother I'm finishing up some business but I'll be there momentarily."

Daniel gave a nod and a slight smile then left and closed the door behind him.

***

"Henry, could you come here a moment?" Mother called as Henry passed her sitting room.

He came and leaned against the door frame. Late morning sunlight streamed through the windows, glowing on the polished wood and creamy rugs. Mother occasionally bemoaned how quickly the sunlight faded the fabrics, but she loved the brightness too much to relocate to a north-facing parlor. She sat at her writing desk, the edge of one beam of light just catching the bottom few inches of her skirt. Letters were strewn across the desk. It was clear she'd only just begun catching up on correspondence.

She ignored the papers, however, and turned to Henry. "Close the door, dear."

Henry had a sinking feeling, but he obediently stepped inside and pulled the door shut behind him. "What can I do for you, Mother?"

"Between the busyness of your sister's first Season and then leaving town, we haven't had a chance to discuss your prospects."

"I beg your pardon?"

"You met several elegant and eligible young ladies in town, and I want to know what you thought of them."

Henry eyed his mother. "I didn't end the Season with an engagement or an attachment. Shouldn't that tell you enough?"

"Not at all. I need to know what displeased you about them, and what you liked, so that I can look for a match that will suit."

"Please don't waste your time on me, Mother. I'm quite capable of finding a wife on my own."

"I have all the time in the world, dear; I can waste however much I like."

"I beg you would not."

"Henry, please. You're the heir. You know as well as anyone that you ought to marry well and extend the line of succession."

"I do," Henry agreed. "But Father's perfectly healthy. I see no reason to rush."

"At least tell me what you're looking for in a wife," she insisted.

He immediately thought of Kate—her bluest of blue eyes and golden hair that never stayed neatly braided back. Her unaffected innocence. The way her smiles made him feel valued for himself as he was, not for what he would inherit in the future.

That was the honest answer to Mother's question. But he had a duty to marry well, and he had a responsibility to protect Kate's secrecy.

He said, "I'll have to think on it."

Mother nodded. "Good. In the meantime, I'm compiling a list of options. You know Lord Townsend has a daughter? Miss Dillinger. She'll be coming out next spring. I hear she's a true diamond of the first water."

Henry forced himself not to scowl. He wanted nothing to do with another spoiled incomparable who expected every member of the *ton* to worship at her dainty feet. "Mother, really—"

"At least *meet* her, Henry. Keep an open mind. We'll have them to tea once we're all settled in town. Can you at least oblige me that much?"

Henry sighed. He loved his mother, and he didn't truly mind that she wanted to help him find a wife. She just had such deplorable taste. In fairness, she was introducing him to the type of girl a duke's heir could be expected to marry. It wasn't her fault they were all missing... something, and he wouldn't be content without it. He'd been doing his best to put her off since he came of age because it was easier simply not to think about it. But Kate... Kate had that something, whatever it was, in spades. If only her background weren't so unconventional.

"Fine. I'll meet her. But I promise nothing more."

Mother gave him a brilliant smile. "Thank you, dear. You may go." She turned back to the letters on her desk.

Henry crossed to her and kissed her cheek, then left the room. Hopefully, she would forget to return to this topic later. He pushed the conversation from his mind. Daniel had challenged him to a friendly shooting competition, and Henry was going to be late.

Chapter 6

Nearly three months had passed since Henry had first brought Hannah to the tower, and other than the one visit they'd missed, they'd returned twice a week. Several times, Hannah had brought art supplies so that the two girls could draw together. Catherine hadn't thought she could enjoy drawing more than she already did, but somehow even the solitary activity was better with a friend. Catherine could feel Henry's eyes on her as she worked, and he always had a ready smile. As she hung her shawl in her window, she wondered what subject Hannah would talk about this week. Sometimes it surprised Catherine that Henry could get a word in, but he must have had years of practice with his vivacious sister.

Henry's shout of "Kate!" outside made her heart skip a beat. No matter how many times they came, his voice made butterflies launch through her. She ran to the window and waved, surprised to see he'd come alone.

When she joined him outside, he stood just beyond the wall, tapping a folded paper in his hand. Catherine had never seen him so discomposed. Excitement and nerves played across his expression, and he flashed a quick, wide grin at her.

"Henry, you look like you can barely contain yourself. What

is going on? Where's Hannah?"

"Mother required her presence for some morning errands today, but I couldn't wait. I've already had to keep this letter to myself for two days."

Catherine glanced at the paper in his hand. "What letter? What does it say?"

Henry unfolded it, his eyes sparkling. "'My dear sir, I do hope this reply is not too late to be of use to your Miss Whitmer, but it took some searching to find what you requested.'" He glanced up at her, faltering. "Is something wrong?"

Catherine blinked. She hadn't heard more than a few words of what he'd read. The brief, initial shock that he'd told someone about her passed quickly at the idea of being *his* Miss Whitmer, as if they were more than friends. The thought sent a tingling sensation through her, but she'd never admit it. "Miss Whitmer," she said instead.

"I'm sorry," Henry said. "I couldn't very well call you Kate when writing to Harborough, though."

With no idea who he was talking about, or even why he'd written, Catherine shrugged. "I know. It's just that *Mama* is Miss Whitmer, not me."

Henry frowned, the letter temporarily forgotten. "Not *Mrs.* Whitmer?"

She shook her head. "She's a spinster." For a moment, Catherine couldn't guess at the thoughts she could practically see swirling through Henry's head, but then she remembered the disgrace and scandal that she'd read about in some of the more dramatic novels Mama had brought home. "I'm adopted," she said quickly.

He stared at her. "You are? I didn't know that."

Catherine shrugged. "Mama won't talk about it, but once in

a while she lets something slip. And we look so entirely unlike that she couldn't possibly be my biological mother. I came to her as a baby." Speaking of letting things slip, Catherine hadn't tried to weasel more details from Mama after the last time she'd accidentally said too much. Perhaps it was time to try again.

Henry shook his head. "I hadn't thought I could be any more intrigued by you, Kate, but it seems I was wrong."

Catherine blushed. She gestured to the letter. "Forgive my distraction. What does the letter say?"

"Oh! Right."

Henry reread the first sentence and then carried on. Catherine's mouth fell open in disbelief at what she heard. Henry's correspondent had found magic that could undo Mama's boundary spell.

"Is it possible?" she whispered.

"Give it a try," Henry said, grinning again as he handed her the letter. "This spell-word will take down the spell and hold it somehow, and then this one—" He moved his finger down the page to another scrawled word, "—will release it back into place again."

"So Mama will never know that I tampered with it?"

"That's the idea." Henry raised one shoulder.

Catherine turned her attention to the letter in her hands. The two spell-words were just legible, and she read them over a few times to hear them in her head. She skimmed the paragraph above one more time to familiarize herself with the rest of the instructions, since she'd been too stunned to take it all in as Henry read it aloud.

Taking a deep breath, she held her right hand out, palm up, fingers spread, as if she were balancing a large ball on that hand. She spoke the first spell-word and held her breath as she felt magic pulling in from all directions to coalesce above her palm, forming a pulsing orb of blue light. She stared at it, amazed. And then she faced a dilemma—where was she to put it? She couldn't carry it around with her. Glancing around, she saw that the nearest bird bath was empty. She carried the weightless orb over and set it gently into the stone bowl. Then she turned back to the garden wall.

Henry waited on the other side, watching her intently, holding his breath. Slowly, Catherine took one step toward the open gate, then another. Step by step, she crossed the invisible boundary. Nothing stopped her. Three steps beyond the border, she froze in astonishment.

"What's wrong?" Henry asked, frowning. "Didn't it work?"

Catherine looked up at him, eyes shining. "Yes!" Suddenly she was moving, flinging herself at him, her arms around his neck, laughing and crying at once. After a startled second, he brought his arms around her waist.

"Thank you," Catherine sobbed softly into his ear. He'd done this for her. He'd opened a door to more freedom than she could remember having. She couldn't put her full gratitude into words, but it consumed her and left her clinging to him more tightly than propriety allowed.

When she'd gotten her breathing under control, she let go and stepped back. Henry pulled out a handkerchief and gently dried her tears. "What shall we do now?"

Catherine looked around. The difference in location was only a few feet, but somehow her perspective from this side of the wall was so very different. The world seemed so much bigger, the possibilities grander. "I don't know," she said.

"I believe you said once that you'd like to ride my horse."

CHAPTER 6

Henry smiled and nodded at Honey. Catherine realized for the first time that Henry hadn't tied the horse to graze when he'd arrived. "Shall we?"

Catherine nodded, eyes wide.

Henry led Honey over then swung himself into the saddle. "We'll have to make do," he said as he reached for her hand. "Step on my foot in the stirrup, and I'll pull you up."

Cautiously, Catherine lifted one foot to rest it on top of Henry's riding boot. Honey was taller than he'd looked from a distance, and it was an awkward position to be in. But Henry reached down for her and lifted her as she pushed herself up, and suddenly she was sitting across Honey's withers in front of Henry. The horse seemed even taller from here, and Catherine was glad of Henry's warm, solid chest against her shoulder and his arms at either side holding the reins. Surely, he wouldn't let her fall.

Henry nudged Honey's sides with his heels, and they moved forward at a slow walk. The motion was strange and unsettling and wonderful.

They passed through the trees, away from the village and prying eyes. Once they reached the open road, a stretch with no houses or farm fields on either side, Henry bent forward to murmur in her ear. "Do you trust me?"

Catherine nodded. She had no idea what he intended, but she had no fear with him.

Suddenly, at a motion from Henry, Honey picked up speed until they were cantering down the road, his hooves thundering against the packed dirt. Catherine bit back a shriek and clutched at Honey's mane, leaning harder against Henry. He wrapped one arm around her waist, the reins still in hand. It gave her a strange sense of safety, even as the countryside rushed past. She found herself laughing as Henry slowed the horse and turned them back toward the tower. Another short canter down the road, then they were walking back through the trees to the garden.

"I'm sorry I daren't take you farther," Henry said, as Honey came to a halt. "Did you enjoy it?"

Catherine was smiling so much she felt like her face might crack in two. "It was amazing."

Henry dismounted from behind her, and for a moment Catherine felt uneasy so high up on the back of the big horse, whose breaths she could feel beneath her. But then Henry was there, reaching up for her. He lifted her down, setting her feet on the ground and supporting her, his hands at her waist, while she gathered herself. She required a lot of gathering, because being so close to Henry was doing something strange to her brain and her heart.

"Th-thank you," she stammered, looking up into his kind face. Her eyes traced the freckles across his nose before meeting his eyes. From here she could see that they were brown with a hint of green around the pupils, not muddy at all but mesmerizing. "I can't express how much... everything... means to me."

"You are most welcome, Kate."

Neither of them moved. Catherine didn't breathe. A whuffle from Honey behind them broke the spell, and Henry let go and stepped back.

"I should go before your mother returns," he said.

Catherine nodded and turned slowly back to the garden. Once within, she scooped the ball of brilliant blue magic into her hand and carried it back to the wall. Speaking the second spell-word from the letter, Catherine gasped as the glowing orb vanished and power rushed outward and away. She reached

CHAPTER 6

across the wall, feeling the boundary spell keeping her in, just as it always had.

Henry, in the saddle again, smiled at her. "Until next time." He turned and rode away

Catherine leaned against the low wall, her knees a little wobbly. She'd thought for a moment, as they'd stood so close, that he might kiss her. But that wasn't something a friend would do. His hesitation was probably nothing beyond concern that she was shaken up from the excitement of the ride. She knew she was naïve and ignorant of social cues, so she must have misread the moment. There was no cause for disappointment, and yet she felt it welling up and dimming the wonder of the day.

It was just as well she had disappointment weighing her down, she decided when Mama returned. Exuberance would have been much harder to hide. Catherine was in low spirits often enough due to loneliness and ennui that Mama barely seemed to notice how quiet she was this afternoon.

The next morning, however, Catherine woke in a brighter frame of mind. Henry and Hannah would come again, and she could use her new freedom to go wherever she wished. The spell-words she'd learned from the letter danced through her head as she washed the breakfast dishes and distracted her as she joined Mama in the library for lessons. Though she suspected most girls her age had left the schoolroom, Mama insisted that Catherine spend a few hours every morning studying. Catherine didn't mind; it gave her something to do, and it was time spent together with Mama. But today it was hard to concentrate.

Catherine had never been one for keeping secrets. She'd never needed to—what in her life had ever required discretion?

What was there in her life that Mama didn't already know? Mama had always been the one keeping her thoughts and feelings close. Catherine had confided everything in her mother, from her childhood wish for a pony to her dream, at fifteen, of dancing at a ball and catching the eye of the handsomest beau.

Her friendship with the Stantons was a grand—and wonderful—secret, and only the fear of losing them enabled her to keep it. Now her glorious freedom bubbled up inside, new and effervescent, feeling so huge that she'd burst with it. She wondered if this was how Mama felt, keeping secrets all the time. Was she constantly on edge, afraid she'd slip up and say something that would give it all away?

And Mama did slip up occasionally. Not often enough to suit Catherine, who wanted to know *every*thing. But enough that she kept asking questions, trying different angles to see what more she could learn. After talking with Henry yesterday, Catherine decided it was time to try again.

"Mama," she began, sitting back and stretching. Her Italian dictionary and the text she was translating lay open on her lap. She'd been working at it for what felt like hours, though she hadn't accomplished much. "Will you tell me again about our family? Tell me about your parents."

Mama smiled as she knit a new pair of stockings. "My mother was from a noble Italian family," she said. "My father was the younger son of a viscount. He went on the Grand Tour of the continent when he finished university before settling down to practice the law with his uncle. He met my mother there, at a ball held by a mutual friend. He was so taken with her that he extended his stay again and again until he convinced her to return with him to England as his wife." Her needles clicking were the only sound for a minute before she went on, "Papa believed in the value of education, and Mama's family were powerful magicians, so I was given not only a comprehensive education but magical training as well. I've tried to do the same for you, Kitty. I know they'd be very proud of you."

Some of Catherine's tension eased as she listened to the familiar story. Her grandparents had died before she'd been born, and she'd never met them, but she hoped they'd love her and be proud of her like Mama said. Now that Mama was in a storytelling mood, Catherine risked another question.

"Will you tell me about when I was a baby?"

This was a subject Mama avoided, and from the long silence that ensued, Catherine expected a change of subject, perhaps a remonstrance to get back to her studying.

But Mama surprised her by saying, "I didn't know the first thing about babies." Her voice and smile were both soft, full of memory. "I'd never been so overwhelmed. You were messy and loud and fragile and constantly hungry. But then you took my finger in your little fist, and you smiled at me. And I knew for the first time what it meant to fall in love." Mama met Catherine's eyes, tears shining in her own. "I knew that I would do anything to keep you—to keep you safe and here with me. Your smile has always been the brightest thing in my life, Kitty."

Catherine rose, setting aside her books, and went to Mama. She sat on the arm of her mother's chair and kissed the top of her head and felt horribly guilty for the secrets she was keeping as Mama laid down her knitting to hug her around the waist. Mama loved her. She must have a reason for her rules. The secrets Mama kept must be so dreadful that she was protecting Catherine from the awfulness.

But Catherine didn't want to be protected. She wanted freedom and choice and a wide-open life. And so she kept her silence, though the secrets gnawed at her belly, and she returned to her lessons.

Chapter 7

Kate was waiting in the garden a few days later. She set aside the book she'd been reading and came to the wall as Henry dismounted.

"Hannah couldn't come today?"

"No," Henry said. "Mother needed her again. But she insisted that I come and take you riding so that your hours of freedom aren't wasted." He was mostly certain that this was a matchmaking attempt of Hannah's, but after Kate's delight at their first ride, he couldn't deny her another opportunity.

"I was thinking of doing something else instead," Kate said before speaking the spell-word that would lift the boundary spell and store it in a glowing orb. He watched her tuck the sphere of blue magic away behind the wall, then remembered that he was supposed to be seeing to Honey. When he'd settled the horse to graze, he met Kate just outside the garden.

"What did you have in mind?" he asked.

"We're going for a walk," she said, smiling up at him. "Come with me."

That smile would get anyone to follow her. They walked together around the garden and into the woods on the far side, away from the direction that he'd come. Kate walked with a light step, practically skipping across last autumn's fallen leaves. It was a hot August day, and though the shade of the trees brought a welcome respite from the sun, Henry was still sweating in his riding coat before long. Kate seemed oblivious to the heat, though the curls that escaped her hair pins clung to her neck and temples.

After several minutes of walking, Henry heard the chatter of a stream nearby, and soon they saw it. Kate clapped with glee and ran forward. Henry followed, noticing that a shallow pool had formed between the mossy banks, calmer than the bubbling brook that flowed above and below it. Kate wasted no time. She plopped herself down on the bank and removed her shoes and stockings, lifting her skirt in one hand as she waded into the pool.

Henry stood frozen, staring. Any other lady showing bare feet and ankles would be shocking, but she was so childlike standing in the water, laughing as it rippled around her. She was something magical at that moment, fae and perfect, and he wondered how he got so lucky as to witness this.

Kate looked up at him impatiently. "Are you coming?"

Henry shook himself and removed his boots and socks, rolling his trouser legs to just below his knees. He stepped toward the water, then paused and removed his coat. If they were going to be dressed inappropriately, he might as well be comfortable. He draped the coat over a low branch before joining her in the pool.

The icy water sent goosebumps across his skin as he waded toward her. Or maybe those were from how she watched him, grinning.

"Wasn't this worth the walk?" she asked.

"More than worth it. How did you know of this place?"

"I used to come here with Mama as a child." She looked

CHAPTER 7

around at the glittering water and rich green moss, then back at Henry. A mischievous light came into her eyes, and she kicked water toward him, splashing the front of his trousers. She giggled. "We used to splash each other until we were both soaked."

Henry, no novice at water fights himself, bent and scooped water at her with his cupped hands. Kate shrieked and tried to run away, slipping a little on the slick stones underfoot. When she straightened, the lower part of her skirt clung to her legs, and drops of water darkened the lavender fabric above. Undaunted, she splashed him again, prompting his retaliation. By the time they'd worn themselves out with splashing and laughing, they were both wet through. Henry averted his eyes as Kate climbed back onto the bank and wrung out her skirt. The wet fabric of her dress hugged her curves all over. He climbed out after her, only glancing up when she spoke.

"Pardon?" he asked.

But she hadn't been speaking to him. It had been a spell-word. Now a strong wind appeared to be flowing from her hand. She waved it over herself, frowning in concentration, until her clothes had gone from sopping to merely damp.

"Would you like...?" She looked at him, gesturing with the wind-producing hand.

"If it's not too much.'

She stepped closer, the wind whipping at his shirt, cravat, and trousers. After a moment, the spell faded, and Kate flopped onto the mossy ground, scratching at her palm. She lay back and watched the dancing leaves of the nearest trees, a contented smile on her face.

Henry lowered himself to sit on the ground nearby but not too close. He rested his arms on his knees and watched the stream burble along. He couldn't look at Kate any longer or he'd end up worshiping at those beautifully bare feet or carrying her off to Gretna Green, where he'd marry her immediately, never to return to her tower prison.

Not that he disliked either idea—his heart pounded its sincere approval—but there was still so much mystery surrounding Kate. She wasn't the woman he ought to pick for his wife, despite the fact that Hannah loved her, and he suspected the rest of his family would as well. His conviction to follow his duty was slipping with every visit, however, as he'd suspected it would. Kate was simply too lovable for his heart to stand.

But even if he was willing to throw caution to the wind and court her in earnest, Kate wasn't ready for that. Ladies got married at eighteen every day, but usually they'd seen something of the world first. He was the first and only man she'd met, one of two new people she'd seen in the past six years. Even if he was ready, which he wasn't, she needed time to know her own heart.

After a few minutes, he asked, "What changed?"

"Hmm?" She sounded dreamy and relaxed.

"You used to come here as a child. You were allowed out of the garden. What changed?"

"I don't know," Kate said softly. "I mean, I can tell you what happened the day before, but I still have no idea *why*."

"What happened?"

"Blackberries."

Henry risked a peek at Kate. Her eyes darted to his and away again.

"I was twelve," she continued. "We were picking blackberries. A boy turned up and joined me. His family's carriage had broken just over on the road, and they'd stopped for emergency repairs. His name was Lucas. He was ten. He stayed to pick berries with me, declaring that his twin brothers kept everyone so distracted that no one would notice he was gone. We had great fun, eating as many berries as we put in the bucket, until Mama came looking for me. She was frantic. I must have wandered farther from her than I should have. When she saw Lucas, she went very still and very white. She sent him back to his family, brought me home, scolded me roundly, and never let me beyond the garden again."

Kate fell silent. Henry didn't know what to say. Her mother's worry over her going missing in the woods was certainly justified, but her reaction seemed extreme. There must have been more going on.

"So you never saw the boy again?"

"No," Kate said. "I doubt I would have anyway—his family was only passing through."

They lounged for a little longer, letting the sun dry their clothes, before tugging stockings and shoes back on and traipsing back to the tower. The mystery that surrounded Kate made her seem even more fae, augmented by the glow of the blue orb of magic she held as she released the spell back into place. Henry half expected her to sprout butterfly wings and flutter up to her tower window without the use of stairs.

***

After the walk to the stream, Hannah came along on every visit. Catherine was delighted to see her friend, but her feelings were muddled. She treasured the time she'd spent with Henry alone, probably more than she should, but she also liked Hannah. Though a year older and more accustomed to the ways of the world, Hannah didn't make Catherine feel foolish or small. She seemed to enjoy the wading pool as much as Catherine did, when another hot day brought them all to the water. There were no splash fights this time, however, and no deep secrets shared.

Sometimes Henry brought along a third horse, saddled like the others, with picnic supplies strapped in place.

"How did you explain this?" Catherine asked the first time. Wouldn't a groom ask questions, saddling three horses when only two were riding? Had they decided to tell their family about her? Should she worry that someone else would reveal their secret to Mama?

"I told the perfect truth," Hannah said with an easy grin. "I'm calling to take my friend on a picnic. She doesn't have a horse of her own, so I've brought one along—this is Blossom, by the bye. Henry, good brother that he is, has agreed to escort us."

Henry grinned at his sister's explanation as he helped Catherine into the new mare's saddle. "I'm starting to wonder what else Hannah gets up to and explains away. She was prepared with that story in less than a minute, I swear."

Catherine would have liked to carry the conversation further, but she was too nervous alone on horseback to speak. Henry showed her how to hold the reins and promised to keep them to a slow walk. He remounted Honey, and Catherine was relieved to see that he held a lead rope attached to her own horse's bridle.

Henry kept his word. They moved at a very slow walk—Catherine could have gone faster on foot—and stopped in a clearing nearby. Henry helped Catherine down, while Hannah dismounted on her own. They had a very pleasant picnic, then Henry suggested a short riding lesson. With Catherine

CHAPTER 7

back in the saddle and Henry holding the lead rope, they walked around the clearing a few times. Catherine still wasn't particularly at ease on horseback without Henry's strong arms around her, but she enjoyed the lesson. She grew more and more comfortable each time they brought Blossom, until she could guide the mare herself, and Henry no longer needed the lead rope.

The end of summer passed, and the weather cooled. Autumn brought brisk winds, golden leaves, and heavy, drenching, frigid rain showers. One Monday morning, Mama hurried out early to the village to reach the shelter of the shops before the rain hit. She hadn't been gone an hour before water pelted from the sky, clattering against the stone pathways in the garden.

Catherine stayed by the stove in the kitchen, unwilling to make up a fire in a second room, but too chilled by the drafts to go without. She had paper and pencils, a book, and a kettle heating on the stove in case she should want tea later. The day may be dreary, but she would keep occupied.

A pounding on the door startled her. She jumped to her feet and hurried over, wrestling the heavy door open, only to gape at Henry, who stood on the steps in the pouring rain.

"May I come in?" he asked, laughing.

Catherine recollected herself and stepped aside for him to enter. "I hadn't thought to see you today." The very few visits he and Hannah missed were generally on days of inclement weather, and this was about as inclement as autumn could get.

As she closed the door, she saw Honey tied beneath the overhang of one of the partially collapsed walls just beside the steps. It wouldn't be as comfortable as a stable, but it could be worse.

Catherine quickly built up the fire. Then she held out her

hand. "Hold still," she told Henry, and cast the wind spell. It didn't do nearly enough to dry his clothing, but it was a start. She took his coat and hung it over the back of a chair. Taking Henry's hand she propelled him to the chair she'd been sitting in near the stove. He surveyed the small round kitchen as she moved about the room, gathering the tea things. Fortunately, the kettle was already hot, and she soon handed Henry a cup of the steaming liquid.

"Won't you have some with me?" he asked when Catherine pulled the other chair out from the table to sit by him.

She shook her head. "Best not. If Mama were to come home before I washed up, I'd rather she only find tea for one."

Henry nodded at the wisdom in this and took a sip.

"I can't believe you rode here in the rain. Didn't Hannah try to convince you not to come? You could catch your death out in weather like this."

He shrugged, his ears going red.

"Why did you come, Henry?" Catherine asked softly. "I hope it's not out of some misguided notion that I cannot be allowed to be lonely. I do look forward to each of your visits, but I can entertain myself on a wet day."

"I know you can. And my reasons were much more selfish."

"Oh?"

He nodded, his gaze fixed on the tea in his cup. "I miss you on the days we don't come—all of them, even when we've just seen you a day or two before."

"You do?" Catherine's voice came out too breathy, and she blushed and searched for something to say so that she wouldn't blurt out how happy she was to hear that. "Tell me about your home. Where would you be now if you hadn't braved the rain?"

"Probably in the sitting room playing backgammon with

CHAPTER 7

Hannah," he said, finally raising his eyes to hers. "Weather like this means my sisters have no callers, and she can only tolerate making over bonnets with Mary for so long." At Catherine's perplexed look, he said, "My youngest sister could play with ribbons and lace all day, constantly refurbishing her already enviable wardrobe."

He described the sitting room and the library, which was where he'd be if his sisters didn't need him. He told her of his mother's parlor that was always bright in the morning, except on days like this when no room was well illuminated. Cauldercrest, he said, had been the home of the Dukes of Caulder since the very first duke six generations ago. It was a grand stone house, but over the generations wings had been added here and there, so that it had a rather irregular layout. Most of the additions had been completed in good taste, however, and the result was charmingly whimsical.

"That's how Mother describes it," Henry said with a shrug. "I'm not sure I'd ever use those words about a house, but I agree. I love Cauldercrest, though we never use all the rooms, not even when our cousins come at Christmas."

Catherine, who had been listening with eager fascination, sighed longingly. "I'd give anything for cousins." She laughed at herself, earning her a grin from Henry. "Siblings, too. I used to beg Mama for a brother or sister, back when I was young and thought they were something she could pick up for me at a village shop." She shook her head ruefully. "I sound like a bit of a goose, don't I?"

Henry chuckled. "No, you sound like a lonely girl who wants a real family."

"I do," Catherine admitted. "A big house full of family is exactly what I've always dreamed of. Siblings, cousins, sundry other relatives..."

"And children of your own?" Henry asked quietly.

"Someday. You? I mean, besides having a title to provide an heir for?"

"Yes," he said. He held his teacup and saucer in his lap, forgotten altogether. His attention was wholly on Catherine, and she blushed. What did he think of her admissions? Was he as uncomfortably aware as she was that he was in a position to give her everything she had ever wanted? It would require more than friendship, though. Did his confession that he often missed her mean he thought of her as more?

To hide her thoughts, Catherine got up and crossed to the window. The rain had lightened somewhat. Above her, the clock in the library marked the hour. She counted the chimes, alarmed at the number.

She whirled, eyes wide, to face Henry. "You have to go," she said, hurrying to him and taking the cup and saucer from his unresisting hands. "The rain has let up, and Mama will be on her way home. She mustn't find you here."

Henry was already on his feet and shrugging on his coat. Catherine walked with him to the door, where he turned and lay a hand on her arm. "Thank you for the tea," he said. "Hannah was sorry to miss you today."

Then he was out the door and leading Honey from beneath the overhanging stone. Catherine watched him out of the garden, waiting for him to disappear into the trees before she shut the door and went to clean up the tea things.

Chapter 8

She was just drying the cup and reaching to put it away when the door opened behind her, startling her so much that she nearly dropped it. She caught it and set it carefully on the shelf before she turned to greet Mama, who had shed her dripping cloak and hung it over a hook behind the door. Catherine's heart was in her throat, her pulse racing. Mama had missed Henry by five minutes.

Recollecting herself quickly, Catherine hurried over to Mama with a towel, using her hip to push the second empty chair back toward its place at the table as she passed.

"Would you like tea, Mama? The kettle's hot."

"Thank you, Kitty. I'll just go change into dry things."

Catherine sagged against the table as her mother disappeared into the upper levels of the tower. She really ought to find a way to tell Mama about Henry. Not only was it the honest thing to do; she didn't know how much longer her heart could take the strain of secrecy.

By the time Mama had come back downstairs, Catherine had a pot of tea and two cups on the table, along with slices of bread and a pot of jam. Mama's dark eyes darted from the tea things to the shelf where Catherine had been putting away the cup she'd washed.

"Didn't you already have tea?"

"Yes," Catherine said quickly. "But I didn't start getting hungry until I was cutting bread for you. And one can never have too much tea on a day like today."

Mama nodded. Catherine didn't like the way her mother studied the chair pulled up before the stove or the still slightly damp stone where Catherine had dried up the puddles from Henry's boots.

Mama looked at Catherine, her gaze sharp enough to cut glass. "Was someone here?"

Catherine's heart froze. She couldn't lie directly to her mother. It was wrong, and it was hard, and her emotions were far too easy to read. She took a deep breath. "Yes," she said, impressed by how calm her voice was. "The son of the Duke of Caulder was out riding and begged shelter from the weather. I didn't dare deny a peer—or a future one, anyway—so I let him sit by the fire and gave him a cup of tea. He left as soon as the rain let up."

Mama's eyes narrowed. "And you didn't think to tell me?"

"Of course I did," Catherine said. "But it seemed reasonable to wait until you were dry and having tea."

One of Mama's eyebrows crept up slightly, but she said no more about it. She sat at the table and allowed Catherine to pour the tea. As they ate bread and jam, they talked about Mama's errands in the village. She hadn't gone to the library, as she couldn't protect the books from rain, but she promised to go when next the weather was fine.

"This rain isn't likely to let up soon, though." Mama frowned at the window. "There's talk of stormy weather for days."

Catherine sighed and waved at her book and art supplies that she'd moved to a shelf out of the way. "We'll keep occupied

CHAPTER 8

indoors," she said. "The kitchen's warm enough at least."

When the tea was finished and cleared away, they settled in for the afternoon. Catherine sketched the things around her: her mother reading in the opposite chair, the stove with the refilled kettle heating on top, the shelves of cups and plates and bowls. She focused on capturing all the little details in an attempt to forget the secrets and half-truths and questions. Did Mama believe her story about Henry's "accidental" visit? Would she tighten the rules and restrictions or add some kind of spell to the tower to keep anyone from stumbling across it? Should Catherine have admitted the whole truth about the man?

No, that last question she could answer easily. Now was not the time to tell Mama about Henry. If Mama didn't like the idea of sheltering a stranger—a duke's son, no less—she would be absolutely livid if Catherine admitted to a clandestine friendship.

The storm had picked up by the time they went up to bed. Wind whistled through the cracks in the shutters. Flashes of lightning lit up the sky, and thunder boomed and rumbled in response. Catherine pulled her blankets up tight to her chin. It took ages to fall asleep, but at last she drifted off, only to wake up to a deafening crack followed by a loud crash. Catherine sat up, disoriented, blind in the darkness.

"Mama?" she called, hating the tremor in her voice.

"Sleep, Kitty," came her mother's voice from below. "You're safe."

"But I heard—"

"Yes, I know. We'll see the damage in the morning. But nothing can hurt the tower spells."

Catherine sighed and lay back down, pulling the blankets

over her head to muffle the pounding of the rain. It was just a storm, it was outside, and they were safe in the tower. She repeated this to herself a few times as she waited for her heart to stop pounding as loudly and rapidly as the rain. After a long, long time, she fell back asleep.

By morning, the rain had settled back to a gray curtain that shrouded the outside world. Catherine met her mother down in the kitchen, but before they prepared breakfast, they went to the door to look outside. Only the door wouldn't open. Something blocked it, something far too heavy to shove against.

"Well," Mama said, straightening after a third attempt to shove the door open.

"We'll have to find another way out," Catherine panted, still leaning against the door.

"Once it stops raining. No sense in forcing our way out just to get wet."

Catherine thought there was a good bit of sense in seeing what was blocking the door and if they could do something about it, but she bit her tongue. Mama wouldn't be going to the village for another two days, and Catherine had nowhere to go. There was no need to rush.

The rain didn't stop until the following morning, the drizzle finally drying up just before noon. Mama leaned out the kitchen window, examining the distance to the ground. She nodded, frowned in concentration, then stepped back and adjusted her glasses.

"Out we go," she said briskly. She positioned one of the wooden chairs in front of the window, stepping up onto it and then the windowsill before climbing through and out.

Catherine crowded to the sill to see what Mama had done. Stretching down along the curved wall of the tower was a

CHAPTER 8

narrow staircase. It appeared insubstantial, formed of cloud or mist, but it had supported Mama as she descended. Catherine picked up her skirts and followed, carefully not looking through the translucent stairs as she went. She looked instead at the garden. It had begun to look drab and brown before the rain, and they'd dug up and composted and winterized it all a week ago. Now the remaining plants lay battered and beaten down and drowning in mud. Catherine sighed and followed Mama around the tower.

The problem was obvious. The section of ruined stone wall that had stood by the door, the section that had sheltered Honey only days ago, had caved in on itself. Several stone blocks the size of Catherine herself had fallen onto the steps outside the door, collapsing the wooden supports and blocking the doorway. Catherine just stared at it. She'd known that the spells that maintained the tower didn't extend to the ruined walls around it, but she'd still expected them to stand as they were for her whole life, and possibly centuries beyond.

Mama stood mutely beside her, studying the damage. "Inconvenient," she murmured finally, when Catherine looked at her. "But there's no damage to the structural integrity of the tower." She turned and began to climb the magical stairs back to the kitchen window.

"But can't you…" She looked between the stone slabs and her mother. Mama had spells for everything. Couldn't she shift the rock somehow so that they could use the door?

"Come, Kitty. I don't want to be washing mud from your hem."

Catherine glanced down at her skirt and quickly lifted it up a few inches. She followed her up the stairs and through the window. By the time Catherine had replaced the chair at the table and glanced back out at the garden, Mama had dissolved the magical staircase.

"Is there a spell that could free the doorway?"

"None that I'm familiar with," Mama said, beginning to gather things for tea.

"Maybe one of your books—"

"We'll make do with the window for now."

Catherine eyed her mother. Finding her own solutions to problems had always been Catherine's method, not necessarily Mama's, but it still seemed odd that she'd give up so easily. On using the only door, no less. Catherine had rarely come across a situation for which Mama didn't know a spell, or know which book to look for it in. So this unhelpfulness, this unwillingness to try, struck Catherine as peculiar indeed.

Was Mama *pleased* that the door was impassable? Could she have…? No. A lightning strike had smashed the wall. Mama couldn't control the weather. Could she?

***

Henry rode urgently toward the tower, Hannah trailing slightly behind him. The sky today was clear and cloudless, though the air was chill. The storm the other night had been something else, fiercer than any Henry had witnessed in years. He'd woken in the dark to the crashing of thunder, and an uneasiness had settled over him. He wanted to know that Kate was safe, but they'd had to wait until her mother would be out.

From the shadow of the trees, he searched first for the shawl in her window. It was there, and he rode forward. He dismounted before reaching the garden wall, however, taking in the damage to the poor remaining plants. Crossing half of

CHAPTER 8

the garden, his eyes fell on the collapsed wall that blocked the door at the same time that Hannah let out a small cry of dismay.

"Kate!" he hollered, worry filling his chest.

Her golden head poked out of the topmost window. "I'll be right down," she called. "Meet me at the kitchen window."

They slowly circumvented the tower, pausing beneath the window he thought was correct, nearly level with the door. Moments later, Kate leaned out. She was smiling and slightly out of breath from rushing down the stairs, and her curls, as usual, escaped from her braid that hung long over her shoulder, giving her a kind of glowing nimbus in the sunlight.

"Are you all right?" Hannah asked.

Kate nodded. "You've seen the damage?"

"Lightning?"

She nodded again. "I'm afraid I can't come out today."

Henry frowned. "How did your mother go out?"

"She conjured a set of stairs from this window." Kate waved between herself and the ground, which had to be a distance of twelve feet or more. "And then she removed the spell before she left."

Henry stared at her. Hannah gasped. "So you can't leave the tower at all while she's gone?"

"Not until I find a spell of my own."

A mischievous light twinkled in her eye, and Henry felt a slow smile spread on his face. This girl wouldn't give up her freedom easily.

"It's odd, though." Kate leaned her elbows on the windowsill and bent forward, as if to shrink the distance between them. Henry took a step nearer, wanting to be closer to her as well. "I'm sure if she wanted to Mama could use a spell to move those stones," she confided. "It's almost as if she's letting the door stay blocked on purpose. Or that she intentionally blocked them."

"Is that even possible?"

"No." Kate scrunched up her face, either because she knew it wasn't possible or because she thought perhaps it might be. "She can't control lightning. Right? But isn't it uncanny that the doorway became impassable the night after you were in the tower?"

A cold chill went through Henry. "Does your mother know about that?"

Kate nodded. "Not everything. But somehow she knew that you'd been here—and, honestly, *how?*—so I told her that the duke's son had been caught in the rain and needed shelter, and that I couldn't very well deny a lord a seat by the stove." She gave a slightly chagrinned smile. "I thought that was enough of the truth without being too much."

"Do you think she didn't believe you? Is that why she's not reopening the door?"

"I don't know. Maybe just a stranger entering the house—me meeting a stranger at all—was enough to spark this." She sighed and rested her chin in her hand. "I wish I could come down there," she mumbled.

"I wish you could too," Hannah agreed. "We could bring rope along next time. I grew up climbing trees with Henry and Daniel, so I'm sure we could climb up if you weren't comfortable climbing down."

"I could climb down from here," Kate said, leaning farther over the sill again to gauge the distance. "But Mama would notice if you came in. Unless…" She glanced up as if she could see through the floors above. "She rarely comes up to my room. But that's a long way to climb."

CHAPTER 8

Henry looked up the tower as it loomed over him. "You work on finding a way to get out from there," he said. Then he grinned. "I'll practice my climbing skills in case it comes to that."

Kate smiled, as if he'd been joking, but he thought he saw a hint of pink in her cheeks. "You'd really climb to the top of the tower just to see me?"

I'd climb to the moon, he wanted to say. He may have resisted pursuing Kate months ago, but by now she owned his heart. She filled his thoughts, and he had a hard time going days without seeing her. If his only chance of spending time with Kate required scaling a tower, he'd do it.

"He would," Hannah said with a grin and a playful elbow to his ribs.

The pink in Kate's cheeks deepened, but for once she didn't look away. There was something in her eyes that called to him. It was a good thing that several yards of distance and a tower wall separated them. If they'd been closer, he couldn't have stopped himself from kissing her, even with his sister looking on.

Kate cleared her throat. "You should go," she said. "Mama probably won't be gone long today."

Nodding, Hannah took Henry's arm and tugged him reluctantly away.

***

Hanging a climbing rope from the stable loft was easy enough. Henry examined it again, tugging on it a couple of times before risking it holding his weight. Kate might have thought he was teasing about climbing up to her window, but he'd been perfectly serious. If she couldn't come out, he'd find a way in. He wouldn't give up the few hours he got to spend in her company because of an obstacle.

It was cold outside, as October began to think about November, and he was wearing shirtsleeves without a coat and old, half-worn-out trousers. He'd warm up soon enough. Henry jumped and caught hold of the rope, wrapping one leg around it and using his feet to clamp it tight. He was in decent shape, but he hadn't climbed much of anything since he and Daniel had had a secret fort in the loft. They'd gotten to it by rope in the same way Henry was doing now. He hauled himself upward, feeling the pull and burn in his shoulders and back. He'd be sore tomorrow.

He touched the ledge of the loft window and let himself back down, then made the climb a second and third time. He stretched as he returned to the house, but he still woke up stiff and aching the next morning. Undaunted, Henry returned to the stable and the rope and made one trip up before deciding to give his shoulders a rest. He'd alternate hard days and easy until he was confident that he could climb the full height of the tower.

He brought a coil of rope along on their next visit to the tower.

The shawl hung from Kate's window, but Henry waited until they were halfway across the dispirited garden before calling. "Kate?"

She appeared in the kitchen window, a bright smile on her face. "I have a spell," she said without preamble.

She held something in her hand, something Henry and Hannah couldn't see from down below. Henry saw Kate's mouth move as she murmured the spell-word, and soon a golden rope had fallen from her window to the ground. She disappeared from the window for a moment, presumably to fasten the top, because when she reappeared, she sat on the window ledge and lowered herself carefully down the rope.

Henry hurried over so that he could catch her if she fell. She didn't, but her arms were shaking by the time she was low enough for Henry to reach up and grasp her waist. He helped her to the ground, neither of them moving as she caught her breath. Henry wanted to wrap his arms around her waist and bury his face in that gorgeous curve of her neck. But Hannah was watching, and he stepped back. Kate turned and stretched her arms and shoulders.

"That was harder than I expected," she said with a grin. "Thanks for your help."

Henry nodded, his throat dry. Kate's cheeks were pink from the cold, and her smile could blind the sun.

"Mama's still acting as if it's immovable," Kate said as she glanced at the rocks blocking the door. She raised an eyebrow, and he knew her suspicions of her mother's motives were only getting stronger.

They stayed in the garden that day, and Henry coached Kate through the climb back into the window, staying close below until she was fully inside. She spoke another spell-word and the rope vanished.

"I'll see you again soon?" Kate leaned out the window, speaking to both of them, but her eyes lingered on Henry, and he felt a warmth in the pit of his stomach.

Hannah assured her that they'd be back at the earliest opportunity. Henry nodded, hoping to silently convey how long that wait would seem.

Chapter 9

"Mama, do you ever wish for brothers or sisters?"

Catherine sat at the kitchen table, one palm propping up her chin as she listlessly doodled on her sketch paper. November had come, cold and dreary, and they had only ventured out for one quick turn about the garden before returning to the warmth of the stove. Catherine had been through eighteen such winters spent with Mama in the small tower rooms, but this year felt lonelier than ever.

"When I was a child, I did." Mama looked up from the book she was reading. "I've long since resigned myself to being an only child. I thought you had too."

Catherine sighed. It was true that she'd stopped telling Mama how badly she wished for a sibling, but that hadn't lessened the longing. Before she could stop herself, she asked, "Do you know anything about the family I came from, before I came to you?"

Mama's eyes widened, her glasses magnifying them until they looked enormous. Her lips pursed. "What other family? *I* am your family."

"But you're not—I mean, you haven't—" Catherine floundered. Mama had never taught her the details of how babies were made, but she knew children required fathers as well as

CHAPTER 9

mothers, and the process was scandalous if the two weren't married. And Mama had never been married.

"No, I haven't, but that doesn't mean you don't belong with me. It's always been just you and me, Kitty, and it always will be." There was a fierce sort of wistfulness to the way Mama said it, and Catherine didn't dare ask any more. A moment later, Mama said, "It's been a few days since you've practiced the harp. Build up the fire in your room and play for a while, please."

Catherine nodded, getting to her feet and heading upstairs. Questions always resulted in spending time in her room. But the questions couldn't be sent away as easily as Catherine. Mama's answers had left her with more questions, but they had also confirmed in Catherine's mind that she was adopted, and that Mama *did* know something about the family she'd come from.

Mama's next trip to town was on a drizzly day. Catherine hung her shawl just inside the window so that the color could be seen but it wouldn't get soaked. She wondered if Henry would come, and if he was serious about climbing the tower. If he hadn't been, she'd go out and they'd walk in the rain, and she'd have to dry her clothes before Mama returned.

She was just wondering what to do while she waited when she heard him in the garden. Looking out, she could see he was already at the base of the tower.

"Kate, will you lower your rope for me?"

"You're serious?"

"I wouldn't ask if I weren't."

Catherine felt a smile pulling at her face as she stepped away from the window and over to her vanity. Plucking a few golden hairs from her hairbrush, she held them together and murmured the spell-word she'd found after hours of searching through Mama's books. The hairs transformed into a thick, golden rope, strong and silky. She secured one end to the nearest bedpost, speaking another spell to hold the knot firm. Then she tossed the free end of the rope out the window, holding her breath as she lowered it, hoping she'd made it long enough. Henry grinned up at her and removed his coat, tucking it into the meager protection of an evergreen shrub. Then he jumped, caught hold of the rope, and began to climb.

Catherine quickly stoked the fire in the hearth and added another log; he'd be soaked and chilled through by the time he reached the top. Then she crossed back to the window to watch. His progress was steady, and as he drew closer, Catherine could see the muscles in his arms and shoulders flex through the wet fabric of his shirt. A corner of her mind told her to stop staring. This wasn't the first time she'd seen him soaking wet and without a coat, after all. And how odd was that—she doubted most young ladies got to see their beaux in such a situation once, let alone several times. Not that he was her beau, she reminded herself. He was her friend. A friend who would climb to the top of an ancient tower just to see her. And a friend who looked rather spectacular doing it. She blushed and turned away, trying to get her heart to stop its fast, irregular beating before he reached her.

She turned back to the window as he hauled himself over the ledge and through, landing panting on the floor for a moment before straightening up. Catherine gaped up at him. He looked like something out of mythology, a godling who had just accomplished a feat of strength. Sweat and rain glistened on his face. He reached up and swiped at it with his sleeve, pushing his dripping hair back and out of his face. His eyes held hers with an intensity that set her stomach fluttering, and she wondered how she'd ever thought his looks ordinary.

He grinned then, breaking the spell, and she reached for the towel from her washstand. She passed it to him, and he made quick work of drying his face and hair.

"Come sit by the fire and dry off," she said.

He followed her across the small room, looking around as he did. There wasn't much to see: the bed, the vanity and washstand, the hearth, the harp. The only seat in the room was a low, velvet-cushioned stool that she moved between the vanity and the harp, depending on where she needed it. She offered it to him, but he shook his head and sat on the stone floor, his legs stretched out in front of him.

"I can't believe you climbed all the way up here," she said, sitting on the stool herself. "Was it hard?"

Henry shrugged. "It's higher than I've ever climbed at once, but I've been practicing." He gave her a little smile that warmed her through.

Catherine suddenly felt shy and uncertain what to say. There was a man in her bedchamber. "How is Hannah?"

"Very well," he said, "though she didn't seem eager to come climbing in the rain with me." He made a face, as though this disinterest perplexed him.

Catherine grinned. "How mystifying."

"And how have you been since I saw you last? Anything new?"

"In the last three days?" She laughed. "You and Hannah are the only new thing in my life in the last *six years*." She looked into the fire for a moment. "Although Mama as good as admitted that I was adopted."

"Really? Wasn't that supposed to be some big secret?"

Catherine nodded. "She still won't tell me anything about the family that I came from, though."

Henry's eyes searched hers. "Do you wonder about them?"

"All the time," she sighed. "I wish I knew what happened to them, and if I ever had siblings. And if… I don't know, perhaps… they might still be alive somewhere." She smiled ruefully. "I know it's unlikely. If they were alive, how would I have ended up with Mama? But if they're dead, why won't she tell me anything?"

"I wish I could solve this mystery for you, Kate."

"Mama's the only one who can do that," she said softly.

They fell silent for a little while, but as always, silences with Henry were comfortable, peaceful, and somehow less empty and lonely than the long stretches of silence with Mama.

"Will you play for me?" Henry nodded to the harp. "I've only ever heard you from the garden."

Catherine flushed. Mama had been her only audience. But could Henry be considered an audience? If silences were comfortable with him, mightn't music be too?

She moved her stool over to the harp and ran her fingers over the strings. She chose a familiar, soft, lilting melody. Henry's unwavering gaze made her nervous, but the music soothed her, and soon she lost herself in it. When the song ended, she played another, and then a third. She didn't once look up at her guest, but she could feel his eyes on her the whole time.

As the last notes of the final song faded, Catherine sat back.

"There are no words to describe how beautiful that was," Henry said, his tone almost reverent. "Thank you."

"You're welcome." Catherine looked around her circular room, feeling like she was coming back to the world from a long distance. She suddenly realized that the fire had burned

CHAPTER 9

down. She jumped to her feet. "You have to go!"

"I'm so sorry." Henry was on his feet instantly. "I lost myself in the music."

Together, they peered out the window. Mama was nowhere to be seen. Henry swung himself through the window, sliding quickly down the rope. Catherine watched him go. With a wave, he turned and disappeared through the garden and into the woods.

Catherine removed her shawl from the window and spoke the spell to get rid of the rope. She used the towel to dry the floor where Henry had left wet footprints, tossing it into the hamper and following up with the wind spell. She watched all traces of her visitor disappear. Building up the fire, she sat back at her harp, determined that Mama should find her practicing when she got home.

Chapter 10

Henry waited impatiently in the carriage for Hannah. They had such a limited window, between the time Kate's mother spent in the village and the snow that threatened. Add to that the fact that their father's brother was due to arrive at any moment with his family, and Henry wanted to make sure that they were well away before any delay could hold them up.

Hannah hurried down the steps, climbing into the carriage and settling across from Henry. He pulled the door shut and banged his hand on the roof to tell the driver to go. Then he looked at his sister.

"You have it, don't you?"

She reached into her pocket for a small box tied with green silk ribbon. It wasn't much of a gift, in Henry's opinion—he'd had about a dozen ideas of things to give Kate that meant more than homemade sweets. He'd even spent free time the last few weeks braiding leather strips into a bracelet and joining them with a tooled square in a floral pattern. But Hannah had argued him out of it. Kate's mother would ask questions if she came across anything new among Kate's belongings, particularly something she wore on her arm. Kate didn't have access to shops or pocket money, either, and an expensive gift, even something as innocent as a book, might make her uncomfortable if she couldn't reciprocate. The last thing Henry wanted was to make Kate unhappy, so he capitulated to his sister's plan. But he kept the bracelet to give her another time, and someday, if he had his way, he'd buy her whatever he wanted.

"It's a good thing you've *always* been an attentive brother," Hannah said, looking out the window. "Otherwise, it would be suspicious how often you escort me on long rides and visits to friends." Her lips twitched as she suppressed a teasing smile.

They had the driver pull up well past the path that led toward the village. They disembarked and tromped through the pathless woods, checking the window for Kate's bright blue shawl as soon as they could see through the trees. It was there, and so was she, framed in the kitchen window, watching for them.

"I didn't know if you'd come," she said after shimmying down the magical golden rope. She wore a navy pelisse over her dress, with a gray woolen shawl overtop, but still she shivered. "The weather didn't look promising."

"It doesn't," Henry agreed, wishing he could hold her close to keep her warm. "But we won't be able to come for the next two weeks because of Christmas guests, and we couldn't risk not getting to see you before they arrive."

Her crestfallen expression wrenched at his heart. "Oh. Of course. The cousins, right?"

"Yes," Hannah laughed. "All of them. Father has an older sister and a younger brother, and they both bring their families for the holidays. It's great fun, and some of them are near enough to our age. I wish you could join us. You'd love it."

Kate's smile looked sad and a little forced. Henry knew

perfectly well that she *would* love it. Of all the gifts he wished he could give her, this was the one he wished for most. "Thank you for coming to see me first," she said. "I have something for each of you."

Henry noticed then that she held two rolled up sheets of paper, each tied with its own blue ribbon. She passed one to each of them, her cheeks glowing pinker when her fingers brushed Henry's. Before they slipped off the ribbons, Hannah gave Kate the box she'd brought.

"This is from both of us," she said. "Mama and I usually make batches and batches of Christmas sweets, but this year we persuaded Henry to help." Hannah grinned up at him. The persuasion hadn't been difficult—after she'd convinced him that all other gifts were impossible, he'd willingly agreed to help make Kate's candy.

They all untied the ribbons at the same time. Kate had given Hannah a sketched portrait that she'd done during one of Hannah's first visits, when they'd sat drawing together. Henry recognized it; he'd spent the entire visit watching Kate work. She had a remarkable skill. Though the likeness wasn't perfect, she'd somehow captured the brightness and enthusiasm that Hannah brought to nearly every endeavor.

Hannah's eyes were wide as she studied it. "You were drawing *me?*"

Kate laughed and shrugged. "You were more interesting than the same flowers I've drawn hundreds of times."

"This is incredible." Hannah hugged her.

Henry's own roll of paper was a watercolor of the pool in the stream. The grass and moss were so green they were practically growing on the page; the sunlight cast mystical shadows across the water. It transported Henry back to their first trip to the stream, when he'd seen Kate barefoot in the water, laughing, and been stunned into entranced stillness. He looked up from the painting to find her watching him. Had she been thinking of the same day when she painted it? He opened his mouth, lost for words.

"It's wonderful," he managed finally. "Thank you."

Kate blushed and opened her own box. She put one of the chocolate confections in her mouth and closed her eyes as she gave a soft sigh of delight.

Hannah jabbed Henry's side with her elbow, and he forced himself to stop staring.

Snow began to fall then, and after a moment of trying to catch flakes on their tongues—Hannah's idea—Kate returned to the tower and Henry and Hannah hurried away, needing to leave before there was enough snow on the ground to leave footprints.

In the carriage, Hannah rounded on him. "Will you just elope with her already? I know it's not the way things ought to be done, but propriety fell by the wayside long before you climbed through her window."

Heat rose through Henry's neck and ears, and he ran his hand through his hair before replacing his hat. He'd climbed into Kate's room three times now. He'd spent hours pondering how to free her from her mother's constraints, and elopement did look like their best option. But a future duchess—because that's what Kate would be—deserved a real wedding in a church, surrounded by family and friends. Kate may be accepted as his choice of wife despite her puzzling background, but no need to add fuel to the gossip fires.

"It's not so simple."

Hannah rolled her eyes. "You've been mad about each other

since we met."

Henry shook his head, not denying but not acquiescing. "I'm the first man she's met. I don't want to take advantage of a childish infatuation."

"Are you saying Kate's childish?"

"No, but naïve, yes. Sheltered, yes. Innocent, yes. I need to give her time."

Hannah sighed. "You're probably right. But it's been months already, and it's frustrating watching the two of you dancing around each other. You're obviously perfect together, and I hate seeing her locked away in that tower any longer."

"I know." It was Henry's turn to sigh.

Chapter 11

It shouldn't have been difficult to go two weeks without seeing her friends. Catherine had lived for six *years* without seeing a single soul besides Mama; surely two weeks would be nothing.

But they weren't nothing. Catherine managed to keep busy and distract herself during Mama's first trip to town during which no one came to visit, but the second seemed to stretch on forever. Catherine sank into an ennui that refused to dissipate even when Mama was at home. They baked a mince pie and ate roast chicken and boiled potatoes for Christmas dinner, but Catherine couldn't work up her usual enthusiasm. She knew that not so very far away, there was a large house full of brothers and sisters and cousins who were probably all laughing and teasing and playing games. Envy was a sin, she knew, and she truly didn't resent the Stantons for having everything. But nothing could stop her from wishing she were there with them instead of trading gifts with Mama. She'd done a watercolor of the view from her window, but she'd given Mama paintings so often in the past that it felt redundant. Mama, in turn, gave her several skeins of the softest golden lambswool to knit a new shawl and a spell book full of illusions.

"It's time for a new challenge," Mama said, regarding Catherine with a look of loving concern. "It's a different form of art. I thought it might lift your winter blues."

Catherine managed a smile. "Thank you, Mama. I look forward to trying them."

She spent much of the next week practicing them. When Mama had gone to the village shops, Catherine lay back on her bed, eating the last of the treats her friends had given her, which she'd hidden deep in her wardrobe. She listlessly filled her room with illusions as her mind circled back again and again to Henry.

She should never have let the Stantons keep visiting. They'd—he'd—ruined her for her life here. Now that she knew what life *could* be like, she would be constantly dissatisfied with hers as it was.

But she couldn't have told them not to come. Each visit was a breath of fresh air, more and more as time went on. At first they had simply been fresh faces, with new stories and new ideas. But Henry was more than that. He was caring and kind, thoughtful, courageous, patient. He was handsome and attentive, and just thinking of him sent warmth all through her.

Did she regret Henry's absence over Christmas because she was bored and lonely? Or did she miss him because she missed *him*?

It had to be the latter. She missed Hannah, too, because Hannah was fun and cheerful, but when the loneliness hit, it wasn't the sister Catherine longed to see. It was always only Henry.

Could she honestly continue to call Henry merely a friend when compared to his sister? Hannah was a friend, and a good one. What she felt for Henry was so much more.

CHAPTER 11

Catherine closed her eyes and let the latest illusion dissolve into empty air. Was this love? Had she fallen for Henry without even noticing? Could he feel the same way for her? And could anything come of it? He was Lord Henry Stanton, heir to the Duke of Caulder. She may be naïve, but she wasn't a complete peagoose. She'd read enough to know that lords didn't marry nobodies. They married ladies with wealth or connections or good breeding, and preferably all of the above. And Henry had access to ladies like these. London was full of specimens of female perfection during the Season. He had no need to settle for a sheltered, provincial adoptee with nothing to offer.

She sighed. Well, she could at least be friends with him still.

***

It was Hannah's voice that called up from the garden the next week. Catherine put her head out the window and waved, then hustled into her pelisse and down the stairs to climb out the kitchen window. Her heart was in her throat. Why had Hannah come alone? Was Henry unwell? She slid down the golden rope and ran to her friend.

"I've missed you!" The two girls met with a warm hug. Catherine stepped back and looked Hannah in the eye. "Is Henry all right?"

Hannah waved off the concern. "He's quite well, but Papa required his assistance on some urgent Caulder business. He couldn't get away, so I left without him." Her eyes twinkled. "I hope you don't mind."

Catherine blushed. "No, not at all, I assure you. I'm so very glad you came."

They set off walking around the garden paths to keep warm.

Catherine asked how Christmas at Cauldercrest had gone, and Hannah launched into a series of amusing anecdotes about the family. Two of the older cousins were married with children of their own, and the five-year-old twins had gotten into more than their fair share of scrapes in two weeks. By the time she'd finished, Catherine felt as if she knew the cousins personally, and she giggled along with Hannah at their antics.

"I expect your holiday was quieter than ours," Hannah said with a glance at Catherine. "I can't tell you how often I wished to escape for an hour or two."

Catherine didn't answer for a moment, listening to their boot steps on the flagstone path. "It was very quiet," she said. "I... I admit, I missed you both much more than I expected. Two weeks should have been easy to bear, but..."

Hannah frowned. "I'm so sorry, Kate. Here I've been, telling you of all the fun you missed. How thoughtless of me."

"No, please, I loved it," Catherine said quickly. "You told it so well that I felt as if I were there."

Hannah's frown lightened somewhat, then returned. "But how will you ever survive when we've gone to town for the Season? We'll be there for at least three months. I could probably feign illness to delay our departure a bit, or possibly even to convince Mama to return home early...."

"Don't even think it. I'd hate for you to miss a minute because of me. You'll just have to remember every detail to tell me when you return."

"If only we could write each other. But I don't know how you'd get the letters to the post."

Catherine shook her head. Correspondence was impossible, though it would have made the distance easier to bear.

They both fell silent for a few minutes. Despite the gloomy

CHAPTER 11

prospect of months without her friends, or perhaps because of it, Catherine couldn't keep her mind from the questions she'd been wrestling with all week. The thought of Henry in town dancing with all the elegant ladies of the *beau monde* made her insides writhe. As Henry's sister, Hannah may not have been the best confidante, but Catherine had no other option.

Hesitantly, she asked, "Do you know what it feels like to fall in love?"

Hannah smiled slyly and looked sidelong at Catherine. "Do you?"

Catherine blushed. "Maybe? I… I think so?"

Hannah's grin widened. "Does this mean you're finally ready to stop pretending that you and Henry are only friends?"

Catherine's face heated even more. "We *are* only friends."

"But you wouldn't mind becoming more." Hannah raised an eyebrow.

"No." Catherine's voice came out just above a whisper. "No, I wouldn't mind."

Hannah laughed. "Don't worry, I won't tell Henry. But I'll tell *you* that he would be overjoyed to learn how you feel."

Catherine's heart lifted. "He would?"

"Oh, yes. There's no other word for it." Hannah linked her arm with Catherine's. "Now tell me more. I'm dying of curiosity."

Catherine let out a small laugh. She felt lighter for sharing her secret with Hannah. If this was friendship, she'd missed out on something wonderful for far too long.

"It probably doesn't mean much to say that he's the best man I've ever met, since I haven't met any others, but he's the best I can imagine meeting as well. He's kind and thoughtful, and he makes me laugh. His smile is, well…" Catherine smiled herself at the thought of how his face transformed into something extraordinary. "And he loves your family more than anything, which is both admirable and adorable." She wouldn't tell his sister how his touch sent shivers through her, or how much she'd loved riding Honey in his arms. Instead, she added, "He makes me feel safe and protected."

Hannah beamed. "I've heard other ladies gush about how wonderful my brother is, but I've never been so delighted to hear it as I am from you. *They* all wanted me to put in a good word for them, but they never truly understood Henry or valued him quite as highly as he deserves." She squeezed Catherine's arm. "*You* do."

Catherine kicked a broken chip of rock off the path in front of her. "Do you think it's love, then?"

"Kate, darling, I've thought it was love from the first time we met. You simply glow whenever Henry looks at you."

Was it possible to catch fire from blushing too much? Catherine *felt* like she lit up when Henry was near, but she hadn't realized that her feelings had been so obvious.

"As I said, your secret's safe with me," Hannah said. "But before you get shy and change the subject, I think you ought to know that I would be beyond happy to have you as my sister. And Mary will, too, once the two of you are introduced."

***

Henry had been under no illusions as to the difficulty of staying away from Kate for two weeks, but even he was surprised by his own restlessness and impatience. The crush of family within Cauldercrest helped; there was nothing like two dozen Stantons to distract a person. But he may have been a bit

CHAPTER 11

shorter tempered than usual, and he sometimes drifted off in thought when he ought to have been paying attention. Hannah was sympathetic, while Daniel laughed at him. His cousin Westley gave him some odd looks, and even Caroline, the mother of the twins, frowned at him when he didn't seem sufficiently amused by their antics.

He'd told Hannah that he needed to give Kate time to understand her feelings, but his confidence in that decision wavered. He didn't know how much longer he could stand waiting before he declared himself. This time apart showed him quite clearly how badly he wanted her in his life, and not just for a few stolen hours a week. He wanted her by his side for the family dinners and the impromptu card parties in the evenings. He wanted to hold her and kiss her with impunity whenever he wished. Naturally a patient person, Henry could wait. But he didn't think he could last much longer without knowing that their feelings and wishes aligned.

Escaping to the stables directly from breakfast, where Hannah didn't even bother fabricating an excuse not to join him, Henry rode a longer, roundabout way to the tower. He needed the fresh air and exercise to calm him before he saw Kate, and he couldn't risk his father calling him into his study to attend to estate business. Not this morning.

A petite figure left the woods on the path to the village as Henry approached, and he gave her a polite nod and kept riding, continuing well past where he would usually turn. The woman could only be Kate's mother, and Henry saw the truth in her statement that they looked entirely unlike. Her mother was dark and small and somewhat plain, the complete opposite of Kate's pale, golden beauty.

Once the elder Miss Whitmer was out of sight, Henry turned

Honey off the road and dismounted, leading him between the trees. A lightning-split tree leaned precariously across their path, and he led Honey around it, wondering if it had been damaged in the same storm that had collapsed the wall near the tower door.

When he emerged from the woods, Henry could see the shawl in the window, but before he could call up, the object of his affections appeared in the kitchen window, scrambling out to slide down the rope. He held his breath until her feet were on the ground, somehow finding himself halfway across the garden without remembering how he got there. She turned and started in surprise to find him there. Then her face lit up like a summer dawn, and everything inside of him turned to jelly. He forgot how to move his feet. He could only stare as she approached and smiled up at him.

"Good morning," she said softly.

He might have nodded in response, or he might have kept staring. Could she have grown *more* beautiful in the last two weeks? Her soft golden curls peeked out from beneath her hood, and those bright, cornflower eyes sparkled. She slipped her hand into the crook of his arm and tugged.

"It's too cold to stand still."

His feet began moving, and he discovered he could breathe again. "I've missed you," he blurted, glad that his voice sounded mostly normal and that the words that had escaped weren't an outright declaration of love.

"Have you?" Her tone was light, almost teasing, but he noticed the hint of pink in her cheeks. "I would have thought that you'd been too busy to miss me. Hannah told me about all the excitement you've had."

"I'm more than capable of missing you no matter how busy I

CHAPTER 11

am," he said. "So Hannah told you about the twins, then?"

Kate laughed. "She did. Their poor mother!"

"What are you talking about? She was egging them on!"

She looked up at him in shock. "No! Really?"

He chuckled. "Hannah may not have noticed, but I know Caroline too well. I'm convinced that half of the boys' ideas were hers to begin with."

Kate laughed, and they fell silent. After a moment, Henry had the sense that Kate's mood had subsided into melancholy.

"Is something troubling you, Kate?"

"It's nothing," she said, but her eyes had lost their sparkle. "Hannah reminded me that you will be in town for the Season. It's not that I didn't know, but…" She sighed. "Three months is significantly longer than two weeks."

Henry's heart sank. He had avoided thinking about London and the *ton* and leaving Kate here, and now his stomach knotted.

"Hannah offered to write," Kate continued, "but it seems impossible. I can't post letters or pick them up in the village without Mama seeing me or hearing about it from someone else."

"No, that wouldn't do." Henry frowned, thinking. Selfishly, he couldn't bear to go the entire Season without even the meager comfort of a letter, and if that was true for him, immersed in the entertainments of the *ton*, how much truer must it be of her.

"If there were a trustworthy person who could receive Hannah's letters and deliver them to me, and who could post my own…" She managed a small, chagrinned smile. "But all of my acquaintance will be in town."

A trustworthy person who would remain in the country

and wouldn't mind aiding a secret correspondence…. A plan formed in Henry's mind, and he picked up his pace, striding eagerly toward the garden wall.

"What—?" Kate began, trotting to keep up.

"I want to show you something."

At the wall, she spoke Harborough's spell and hid the glowing blue sphere beneath the bare azalea bushes. Henry took her hand and tugged her toward the woods. His heart thudded faster at how perfectly her small hand fit within his.

They stopped at the lightning-split tree.

"Oh," Kate breathed, stepping closer to lay her free hand on the rough gray bark. "The storm must have done this."

"Yes. Look." Henry pointed to where one branch had been sheared away, leaving a small, hollow gap in the wood. Kate looked from it to him, confused.

"This will be where your post is delivered," Henry said. "Hannah will direct her letters to our housekeeper, an excellent woman who loves a good intrigue. Mrs. Knight will then send a footman to place the letters here. That way, we don't have to worry about them arriving at the wrong time or on the wrong day or giving away the secret. This tree is hidden both from the tower and from the path to the village, and the hollow place will shelter the paper from foul weather. Then, when your mother is out, you can come retrieve them and leave any you'd like to send Hannah in return."

Kate's face brightened by degrees as Henry spoke, until they were both grinning like children.

"How perfect!" She squeezed his hand, and he squeezed hers back. "I *knew* you'd help me find a solution."

Her praise made his chest swell, but there were still unsolved problems that ate at him. The greatest being that they would

CHAPTER 11

soon return to the tower where she would climb up her magical rope and disappear inside, while he rode away.

Chapter 12

Catherine chose to ignore the passage of January and February. Time hardly seemed to exist in the tower at the best of times, and Henry's impending departure was far from the best. They went about their visits as usual, mostly with Catherine climbing out of the kitchen window, but sometimes with Henry climbing all the way up to sit by her fire and talk. When she did think of the coming Season, she tried to focus on the good, on how Henry had arranged for her to send and receive letters to her friends.

Hannah said her goodbyes on the last Monday of February, as their mother would need her assistance with planning and preparing for their trip. Henry returned alone on Thursday. The day was unseasonably mild, and they wandered through the woods hand in hand.

As they passed the damaged tree that would soon prove so important, Henry said, "I've told Hannah of our plan. She'll write at least once a week, and she promised that they would be long and full of detail."

Catherine smiled. Hannah had assured her of that as well.

"Do you think…" Henry hesitated, and Catherine could see the telltale red of embarrassment in his ears. "Would you mind if I enclosed a letter every so often?"

CHAPTER 12

"Would I mind!" It baffled Catherine that he would be shy or embarrassed to ask that. Or that he felt the need to ask at all.

"I know that I'm not your betrothed, and it's not quite the thing, but I thought maybe… since the correspondence is already clandestine…"

With a confusing swoop in her gut, Catherine understood. She hadn't known that only engaged couples could write. Mama had evidently not seen the need to tell her that, as she seemed determined that Catherine should have no one to write to. Did his asking mean that betrothal was on his mind?

She turned to Henry and took his hand in both of hers. "Henry, I would love to receive letters from you."

His eyes were intense as they searched hers. She noticed that flecks of gold had surfaced in the brown and green, and she wondered what that meant. Had she somehow missed them before? Or did they only appear when he was held by a strong emotion? If the latter, what was he feeling so keenly? Her stomach fluttered.

When they returned to the garden, they hesitated in the shadow of the tower. Catherine didn't want to climb back in. Not yet. Tears pricked at the backs of her eyes. Henry would be gone for months, and he would often be in the company of diamonds of the first water, all of whom would find him a matrimonial prize. He wouldn't forget her, would he?

She bit her lip. She wished her voice to come out light and cheerful, but it quavered. "Think about me sometimes?"

"I'll think of you every moment of every day, Kate."

His voice was low and rough with emotion. A tear slipped from the corner of her eye, and he raised a hand to cup her cheek and swipe the tear away with his thumb. Catherine's heart and lungs were behaving erratically, and she couldn't catch a breath as he lowered his face slowly toward hers. His other arm slipped around her waist, pulling her close as he kissed her. His lips were soft, tender, full of longing, and Catherine melted. She would have been a puddle at his feet if his arms weren't there to support her. When he broke the kiss, he only pulled back an inch or two, just enough to look at her. His eyes flickered with gold.

"Merciful heaven," she whispered. That kiss had successfully banished any lingering doubts about whether this was love or friendship.

Henry chuckled and pressed one more light, quick kiss to her lips. "I'll be back," he promised. "As soon as I can."

Catherine nodded and watched him go. He turned and waved before vanishing into the trees.

***

Catherine was sitting at the kitchen table with a cup of tea and a book when Mama came home. Mama glanced at her briefly as she removed her cloak, spencer, and gloves, then froze and gave her another, sharper look.

"You've been kissed."

Catherine's mouth fell open as she stared at her mother.

Mama scowled. "Don't gape at me like a fish, Kitty. Who was it? Who did this to you?"

Catherine closed her mouth. Her heart galloped as she tried to feign ignorance. "How could you—why would you—?" She spluttered faintly.

"A mother knows." Mama strode over and took Catherine's chin in her hand, tilting her head this way and that, as if she could see lingering traces. Perhaps she could. *"Who was it?"*

CHAPTER 12

she demanded, slow and dangerous.

Never once had Catherine had a reference point for the word *livid*, but now she comprehended it. Mama was livid. Furious. Incensed. Catherine shrank away, pressing against the back of the chair. She couldn't think of a single thing to say.

"It was that duke's son, wasn't it?" Mama's eyes narrowed. "The one you foolishly sheltered from the rain?"

Catherine had become a statue, unable to nod or shake her head. Her eyes must have held the answer, however. Mama let go of her chin and reached for her cloak, muttering. The thought of Mama going after Henry broke Catherine from her stupor.

"No, Mama, don't. He's gone. He was leaving for town for the Season." Her mother paused, half turned to look over her shoulder. "It won't happen again. Truly."

It wouldn't happen for at least three months, but she'd be perjuring herself most severely if she said she didn't *want* to kiss Henry again.

Slowly, Mama hung her cloak back on the hook. "For the Season? Good. He'll meet someone new, and you will be forgotten."

Catherine's heart seemed to stutter to a stop. Mama had given voice to Catherine's greatest fear, and she'd spoken as if it were a desirable outcome. Catherine's stomach knotted and twisted, and she thought she might be ill.

"Why, Mama?" she asked softly, pressing a hand flat against her belly to quell the churning. "What is so terrible about a gentleman showing interest in me?"

Mama sighed and sank into the other chair. "I'm trying to protect you, Kitty. Everything I do is to protect you."

"Are you sure you're not selfishly trying to keep me to

yourself?" Catherine clapped a hand over her mouth. She'd never talked back to Mama, not in years. Thoughts like these had certainly crossed her mind, but she'd never spoken them aloud. She looked apprehensively at Mama.

Her mother's mouth tightened into a thin line, and her eyes went hard and cold. "You have no idea what men are capable of. Even illustrious, upstanding gentlemen are snakes in the grass."

Catherine frowned. "What do you mean?"

Mama sighed, and some of the tightness went out of her face. "I *chose* spinsterhood, Kitty. Yes, I'm plain, but I had offers. I'd hoped never to tell you this story. I'd hoped you'd trust me to bear your best interests in mind. But it seems you must hear it."

"Hear what?" Catherine whispered.

"When I was in my third Season, a young lord pursued me—a newly made earl, with a fortune and a grand estate and a library that could have kept me busy for years. I thought he loved me. I thought he enjoyed my conversation and appreciated my intellect; I even believed that he found me lovely. I was certain that *I* loved *him*." Mama pressed her lips together and took a sharp breath in through her nose. "But I was wrong. On all counts. All he wanted from me... hm, well, he wanted the eggs without buying the chicken. He had no intention of marrying me, only using me and abandoning me. My best friend's older brother heard him laughing about it at their club, and she told me. I confronted him. He defended himself admirably, with fawning endearments, and I forgave him. The next week, he'd moved on, pursuing a young heiress with a pretty face and a negligent guardian." She raised her eyebrows and fixed Catherine with a fierce look. "Men cannot be trusted."

CHAPTER 12

It took nearly a full minute before Catherine could speak. "But what about your father? Wasn't he trustworthy? They cannot *all* be horrid."

Mama's eyes softened. "My father was the best of men, and unfailingly loyal to Mama and me. I have never met another like him." Her mouth softened, too, into a slight smile. "You're all I have, Kitty. I would give anything to protect you from experiencing the heartbreak and humiliation I went through. I *do* want to keep you here with me, but not out of selfishness. You are safest here with me. We are an inseparable team, at our best when we're together."

Catherine dropped her gaze to her tepid tea and said nothing. She wouldn't be convinced that Mama wasn't motivated at least in part by self-interest, to have a companion in spinsterhood. Nor did she believe that *she* was at her best with Mama. No, Henry brought out a lightness and a boldness in her that she'd never felt before. But there was no point arguing. Henry was leaving. It was wiser to submit quietly and meekly accept Mama's assertions. Bridges could be crossed when—if—they came in three months.

Chapter 13

Hannah's first letter to Kate, written less than a week after their arrival at Caulder House in Berkeley Square, was full of the same happy chatter that Hannah could produce at a moment's notice. She showed it to Henry, and once he'd read beyond her assurances of their safe arrival, he skimmed the rest. There were too many descriptions of shopping for new gowns, bonnets, and gloves, and trying to find ribbons that matched a favorite gown. That had been how the ladies of the family had spent their first week, in between social calls from Mother's friends. The Duchess of Caulder had a vast acquaintance, and several were already in town. Henry avoided the drawing room most mornings. Mother hadn't mentioned her hopes of finding him a wife again, but he knew better than to think she'd forgotten. She was looking for a match for Hannah, too, and the social calls over tea and cake were an uncomfortable cross between matchmaking and spouse shopping. No wonder the *ton* used the phrase Marriage Mart to describe their efforts.

He offered to drive Hannah and Mary through Hyde Park in the phaeton, and though spring had not yet caught hold, they both eagerly accepted. Hannah had no patience for gossipy older ladies, and Mary grasped at any break from the

CHAPTER 13

schoolroom and her governess, who had traveled with them to London.

Hannah mentioned the drives in her letter to Kate, and suggested that when they were back in the country for the summer, they should take Kate out so that she could experience the phaeton.

"I don't know why I didn't think of it before," she wrote, "and I hope you'll forgive the oversight."

She'd left him just enough space to add a brief line at the bottom about how he'd never found London so dull as he had that week. He hoped that Kate would take it not only as a teasing jab at his sister's excessive shopping, which it was, but also as a hint that he missed her. Hannah enclosed the letter within another to Mrs. Knight and left it on the butler's silver tray to post.

A letter arrived from Cauldercrest a few days later. The date on the letter showed that it had been written before Kate had received Hannah's—the footman must have picked it up from the tree when he left Hannah's for her. Hannah read it silently at breakfast, a small furrow creasing her brow. She folded the letter and applied herself to her tea and kippers. When she'd finished eating, she rose and gave Henry a significant look. He followed her from the room. She took refuge in the library, where they'd be undisturbed. When Henry closed the door behind them, she took the letter from her pocket and held it out to him.

"Perhaps you can understand what she's talking about better than I," she said. She watched him unfold the letter and begin to read.

It wasn't long, only one side of a half sheet of paper. Kate's handwriting was round and loopy and easy to read, as open and unaffected as she was herself. Henry smiled just looking at it.

"I do hope you've arrived in safety," Kate wrote, "and that everything is coming together for a successful Season. I know you've done it all before, Hannah, but you seemed a trifle apprehensive before you left, and I thought I ought to tell you that only fools will fail to appreciate you. You're lively and vibrant and loyal, and if anyone will take a moment to get to know you, they'll be knocked off their feet."

He glanced at Hannah. Nothing in what he'd read so far could be confusing. She nodded at the letter, and he returned to his reading.

"On another matter, you both might be interested to hear that somehow Mama knew without being told how Henry said goodbye. I'm baffled by this, but it must be what they call a mother's intuition. She's barely let me out of her sight since that day, and she's rearranged her trips into the village so that she only goes once a week on variable days. I'm more grateful than ever for the lightning tree because it would be nearly impossible for letters to be delivered otherwise. I am perfectly well, however, and still able to escape the tower when she *does* go out. Please assure Henry that I have no regrets. He is absolutely *not* to feel guilty. If I read a single word of self-recrimination, I shall refuse to write again."

Henry's brows drew together as he read. His stomach sank to his toes. Kate could forbid his guilt, but she couldn't banish it. She'd lost a measure of freedom, and it was his fault. Slowly, he raised his eyes to Hannah's.

"How did you say goodbye, Henry?"

The corners of her mouth twitched as she suppressed a smile. How could she find this amusing? Kate's home situation had

CHAPTER 13

become more complicated than ever. He scowled at her.

Her eyes twinkled. "You kissed her, didn't you?"

He ran a hand through his hair. "I wasn't thinking."

"I'm sure you weren't," his sister agreed. "I'm sure your heart made that decision, not your head." She grinned. "Do you regret it?"

He ought to. He should never have put Kate in that position. But he answered truthfully. "No. If she were here, I'd do it again."

"And again and again, I suspect," Hannah giggled. Henry's ears grew hot. "I did tell you to elope with her months ago." She took the letter from Henry's hand and patted him on the arm. "She doesn't regret it either, so forgive yourself for not being prescient and carry on. Her situation is not so very much worse than before. She can still get our letters." She smiled and moved to leave the room.

Henry stopped her. "For what it's worth, I agree with her. Only a fool would overlook your value, and you know I'm not referring to your title or dowry."

Her smile widened just a bit, and she quietly slipped out of the library.

***

"Thank goodness it's so wet today."

Henry stared blankly at his mother. Her pronouncement was entirely out of character for the woman who spent most of her time in the sunniest room in Cauldercrest. She lifted her cup of chocolate to her lips and eyed him over the rim. After a long, slow sip, she lowered the china cup and smiled at him.

"I've invited guests to take tea this morning, and I expect you and Hannah both to be there. The Good Lord has conspired with me, it seems, to keep you from driving out today."

Henry stifled a sigh. "Who are your guests, Mother?"

"Lady Townsend and her daughter, Miss Dillinger." She arched a delicate brow. "I mentioned her to you before—do you remember? You agreed to meet her and keep an open mind."

"I remember agreeing to meet her," Henry answered grudgingly. "But I promised nothing beyond that. I wish you would leave off matchmaking. Put your focus on Hannah, not me."

The duchess gestured vaguely with the hand not holding the cup of chocolate. "My work for Hannah will be carried out at balls and dinner parties. You can be certain I won't neglect her."

The daughter in question entered the breakfast room then, followed by Mary, who was pleading with Hannah to come with her to the milliner's to take another look at particularly fetching bonnet. "It would look darling on you, I'm sure, Hannah," she said, helping herself to a cup of chocolate.

Mother didn't give Hannah a chance to respond. "Not today, Mary. Your sister will be having tea with Henry and me this morning."

Hannah and Mary both looked at her in surprise. "Who's coming?" Mary asked bluntly. "A suitor?"

"No, dear, we'll begin expecting them after Lady Sefton's ball next week. Lady Townsend and Miss Dillinger will be joining us. Miss Dillinger has been universally described as a diamond of the first water, and she's about your age, Hannah. It wouldn't hurt to make friends with her."

Henry saw Hannah's lips tighten slightly before she nodded and poured herself chocolate. As she drank, she shot Henry a look. He raised one shoulder slightly in a shrug. Neither of them were especially fond of Incomparables, the *crème de la crème* of young ladies entering the *beau monde*. They were almost uniformly vacuous and vain, with a strong sense of entitlement, regardless of whether they actually possessed a title.

Later that morning, when the ladies had arrived and Mother sent for Henry to join them in the drawing room, Hannah caught him outside the door.

"You're actually going along with this?" she hissed. "Mama didn't bring Miss Dillinger here to matchmake a friendship for me."

Henry shook his head. "She badgered me into agreeing to meet her months ago, but I've reminded her several times that I promise nothing more than that."

"You ought to tell her about Kate. She'll get her hopes up about each potentially perfect match she finds, and you'll disappoint her time and time again."

"Not right now. We have company. Or do you want to create an even bigger scene than Mother could make on her own?"

He could see Hannah weighing the value of announcing Henry's attachment to another young lady in front of a potential match. It could be amusing, but then not only would Kate no longer be secret, she'd be the talk of the *ton*, and it was bound to get back to her mother and cause problems.

"Soon, then," Hannah muttered.

They entered the drawing room together. Mother made the introductions. Miss Dillinger was tall and willowy with smooth auburn hair and startling violet eyes. Her mother was somewhat shorter, and her rosy hair was streaked with silver, but other than that they looked a great deal alike. Both greeted him with gleaming smiles. Henry could feel his mother watching him as he bowed politely and took a chair opposite Miss Dillinger. He could sense the disappointment from all three ladies that he hadn't chosen the open seat beside her. Hannah smirked and took it herself, giving him an arch look that suggested he'd owe her a drive through the park or another favor in return.

"Tell me about yourself," Hannah said with a disarming smile. "Do you draw? Do you play?"

"Both. I'm not much of a painter, but I'm rather good at playing duets. You?"

"My sister Mary and I play duets occasionally, but only for fun. I confess, too many fingers on the pianoforte can be confusing."

"Perhaps playing with a younger sister is the problem," Miss Dillinger said brightly. "We should play together. Your brother can judge our success." She turned her smile on Henry again.

"I'm no judge of music," he said, keeping his own expression cool and polite.

Hannah changed the subject, bringing up, in turn, dancing, books, and whether they enjoyed the theater. Miss Dillinger *adored* dancing, had nothing to say about books, unless it was to praise the latest novel by Mrs. Radcliffe, and attended the theater as often as she could. She said all this without once letting her brilliant smile falter, fluttering her long lashes at Henry every minute or two.

The affectations of the ladies of the *ton* were nothing new to Henry. Ever since he came of age, young ladies with an eye for a duchy were trying to snare him. He'd survived three seasons of the nonsense, and he'd thought he'd grown inured to it. It was a hazard of his birthright. But having spent time with Kate, with her refreshing candor and simplicity, Miss Dillinger's coquetry was like a cloying, choking perfume. This was the kind of young woman his mother thought he should marry? His stomach turned, and he wished he could excuse himself from the room.

The two mothers were speaking quietly together, but anyone could tell they were watching the exchange avidly. Henry contented himself with exchanging a look with Hannah.

She turned back to their guest. "What of magic? I always admire ladies who count magic among their accomplishments, as I have no skill for it whatever."

"I'm afraid we're alike in that," Miss Dillinger said with a pout.

When Henry and Hannah exchanged another glance, Mother spoke up to join their conversation. "Nothing to feel badly about, dear. We're a notoriously non-magical family." She fixed Henry with a sharp stare. He ought to have gallantly offered her that comfort himself, but he wouldn't play this game. He had no intention of giving Miss Dillinger a false idea of his level of interest.

The rest of tea passed politely but awkwardly. The two mothers carried on half the conversation, with Hannah and Miss Dillinger chiming in. Henry kept silent unless called upon specifically. Miss Dillinger seemed to notice this, so her remarks as time went on increasingly included appeals to Henry for his opinion.

At last, the ladies rose to leave. Henry bowed silently, leaving his mother to utter the requisite polite nothings. She followed their guests to the door, while Henry and Hannah stayed in the drawing room. As soon as their guests were out of earshot, Hannah flopped onto the couch and flung her arm over her eyes.

"How exhausting," she groaned. "You didn't even *try* to carry your weight in the conversation."

"If I had, she'd have gotten the wrong idea." He stood and stretched and walked to the hearth, where he frowned down into the fire.

"You're quite right, but I think you may owe me a *week* of phaeton rides for this."

Henry chuckled. The sound died on his lips as his mother entered.

"You agreed to have an open mind, Henry," she accused, stalking over to him, her face set and stern. "Your behavior today was far from the charm and humor I've come to expect from you."

"I agreed to meet her, Mother, and I have. I didn't find anything to admire in her, so I would appreciate it if you would drop the issue."

"Nothing to admire!" Mother threw up her hands. "She's exquisite, and surely you noticed those eyes! She's accomplished, poised, and a much better conversationalist than most young ladies straight from the schoolroom. What more could you want?"

Hannah raised her arm from her face and eyed him meaningfully. But Henry was too put out by the whole situation to tell Mother about Kate. He'd spent his adult life expecting to marry an Incomparable, someone who would do justice to the title of duchess, and he knew that was what his parents expected of him. They expected him to choose a woman with potential and let love grow after marriage into the kind of warmth they shared. But he'd had hope since meeting Kate that there could be more depth to the relationship. Looking into his mother's

CHAPTER 13

flashing eyes, however, he doubted himself—he did not doubt that he wanted Kate above all, but he questioned how his family would react to the choice, and whether love really could, and should, trump duty.

In any case, informing his mother about his secret, unofficial courtship of his true love was not something to undertake when they were both in a foul mood.

"We'll discuss it later, Mother. I'm going out."

He left them both staring after him. He was already halfway to Gentleman Jackson's before he began to feel guilty for his rudeness. Hopefully, a bout in the ring would work off his frustration.

Chapter 14

Lady Sefton's ball, the first big event of the Season, was a proper crush. Everyone seemed to have arrived in town in time to attend. The drawing room, dining room, and salon overflowed with people. Music came from the drawing room, where the furniture had been removed to make space for dancing. It was a wonder that anyone could dance at all in this crowd. Henry could barely squeeze through. He saw his father disappear into the throng in search of the room set up for card players. Mother, towing a wide-eyed Hannah by the hand, set off to greet her acquaintance and take up a position near the drawing room doorway, where Hannah would be seen and asked to dance.

Henry began to wend his way in the opposite direction, grateful to find a spot to stand near the open window of the dining room. From across the room, a friend hailed him. Henry raised a hand but made no attempt to leave his post. As predicted, a few minutes later, the man joined him. Nathaniel Johnson, heir to the Earl of Bembry, handed Henry a cup of lukewarm punch.

"Thought I'd see you here," Johnson said.

Johnson was tall, fair, and handsome. He was a bit of a flirt but a harmless one, and he'd been one of Henry's closest friends

CHAPTER 14

for years.

"Her Grace has Lady Hannah dancing?"

"If she isn't already, she will be soon." Henry took a sip of his punch. "If you want to get on her dance card, now would be the time to ask."

Johnson glanced toward the drawing room but shook his head. "It's too loud. We wouldn't be able to hear each other, and my conversation is what makes my dancing tolerable."

Henry grinned. Johnson *was* a subpar dancer. He was an ace with his fists and a bruising rider, but the moment music played, he lost all coordination.

"You should dance, though. There are some real beauties in the crowd tonight."

Johnson surveyed the crowd, and Henry followed his glance. His gaze fell on Miss Dillinger, who was watching him with those amethyst eyes. She smiled coyly and fluttered her lashes. Henry looked away, his grin fading. Two other ladies tried to catch his attention, both dark-haired and pretty. He dropped his gaze to his punch cup and took another swallow.

"I hate dancing in crushes like this," he told Johnson. "You're welcome to go, but I have no interest in having my toes stepped on or taking an elbow to the side every time I turn around."

Johnson chuckled. "It is a bizarre pastime, isn't it?"

"This coming from a man who willingly takes a pummeling in the name of exercise."

"I do not," Johnson protested. "I give as good as I get, and better, usually."

The two stayed by the window for the rest of the evening, greeting acquaintances as they passed through for refreshments. Escorting Hannah out to the carriage afterward, Henry said, "Did you dance the whole evening, then?"

"Most of it," she said, breathless and glistening with sweat. "I don't have high hopes for any of them, but it was nice to dance, and the company was pleasant. Where were you?"

"Standing by a window with Johnson."

"I could have used a window." Hannah brought a handkerchief to her temples. She glanced sidelong at Henry. "Johnson was here?"

Henry knew that she was surprised that his friend hadn't danced with her. At all the balls they'd mutually attended last Season, he'd asked for at least one dance, often two.

"He didn't think his dancing skills would display well in such a crush."

Hannah rolled her eyes and shook her head. "Nonsensical man." She paused. "Was that your excuse as well?"

"For not dancing with you? I would have thought you had much better partners."

"For not dancing with *anyone*, Henry. Mama is quite put out."

Henry sighed. He'd known she would be. "I don't want to encourage them."

Hannah squeezed his arm, but by then they'd reached the carriage, and their parents were waiting. Henry handed her in and then slid next to her on the seat.

"You didn't dance, Henry," Mother said, frowning at him.

"Neither did Father," Henry pointed out.

"He's married with children; he doesn't need to. *You* are still on the market."

"Mama," Hannah said, "You know how much Henry dislikes dancing in such tight quarters. One hardly has room to breathe."

Mother pursed her lips but didn't dispute the fact. Father took her hand in his, and she glanced at him, her expression

CHAPTER 14

softening.

"Very well, I'll forgive you this once. But we're attending Almack's next week, and I expect you to dance."

Henry turned his attention out the window, watching the dimly lamplit streets roll by. He dearly wanted moments like his parents just shared, ordinary moments of togetherness and understanding, with Kate. He wanted to take her hand, share a look, sit beside her every day for the rest of their lives. But duty and expectations settled like a weight on his shoulders.

***

Once the Season had been kicked off by Lady Sefton's ball, there were dinners and parties and musicales nearly every night. Henry wished that he could get out of attending most of them like his father did, but Father was probably only so fortunate because he had a grown son to escort the ladies of the house in his place. Mother wanted Henry to go, so Henry must go.

They both attended Lord and Lady Haseltine's dinner. Lord Haseltine was a distant cousin, and he and Father stood by the mantle discussing their hunting and fishing successes of the last year while they waited for dinner to be announced. Mother and Lady Haseltine sat side by side on a sofa, talking in low voices. Their daughter was Daniel's age, two years older than Hannah. Henry had always found her to be friendly but vapid, and judging by the somewhat pained look on Hannah's face, she still was. Another young lady sat with them, a Miss Quill, who was staying with the Haseltine family for a fortnight. She had a pleasant, heart-shaped face and light brown curls that bounced when she shook her head animatedly at something

Hannah said.

Henry sat with Johnson and the new Lord Wortle. Wortle had been Jack Chivers when Henry had known him at university, a short and stocky fellow with pale blue eyes and a wide mouth. He smiled easily and talked too much. He'd inherited the Wortle title from his grandfather less than a month ago.

Henry listened to his friends talk, alternating between studying the mothers and the daughters. He had a strong suspicion that the duchess and the viscountess had carefully planned the guest list for this dinner. Three unattached young ladies of good families; three single young men who either had titles or would inherit them. Miss Quill wasn't the usual diamond his mother encouraged him to pursue, but that didn't mean much.

When the final members of the party were announced, and Lady Townsend and Miss Dillinger entered the drawing room, Henry's suspicions were confirmed. This dinner was held entirely for matchmaking purposes. With effort, Henry schooled his features to avoid showing his distaste for the idea. He wanted Hannah to find a good match, and he knew Johnson admired her. He wished the others all the best. He just wanted no part in it.

At dinner, Henry found himself seated between Miss Dillinger and Miss Quill, as expected. He shot his mother a sharp glare, which she ignored. Hannah, seated next to Wortle, smiled at Henry across the table in a mix of amusement and sympathy. It was a chatty company, with several discussions going at once, and Miss Dillinger didn't hesitate to attempt to draw him into conversation. She was having a lively debate with Johnson about whether the fluffy little dogs preferred by the ladies of the *ton* actually qualified as dogs at all. Johnson

CHAPTER 14

teasingly maintained that only hunting dogs deserved the name.

"Do take my side, Lord Henry," Miss Dillinger pouted. "Perhaps you can convince Mr. Johnson that dogs are good for companionship as well as hunting."

Henry had no intention of taking anyone's side. "I don't keep dogs, myself," he said coolly. "I have no opinion on the matter." He turned to Miss Quill and said something vague in compliment of the soup.

While that maneuver extracted him from Miss Dillinger's debate with Johnson, it opened him up to Miss Quill asking him if he enjoyed books. Henry replied that he did enjoy reading, while silently remembering one of his early conversations with Kate about reading history and William the Conqueror. Miss Quill gushed about her own literary delight. He listened with half an ear, keeping his eyes on his plate or on his sister across the way. Poor Hannah was just barely hiding her dismay at her dinner companion. Wortle was too much of a rattle to suit Hannah. If only Henry could have traded places with the man; Wortle and Miss Quill might have done nicely together.

When the ladies finally retired to the drawing room, leaving the gentlemen to port and brandy, Johnson leaned over to Henry. "You've been quiet this evening."

"Nothing much to say." Henry shrugged.

"That's unlike you."

"I'm not a rattle like Wortle," Henry said quietly, so that only Johnson would hear.

"No, but you can converse nearly as charmingly as I can." Johnson grinned. "One would think that having a lovely young lady on either side would bring out your best, not your worst."

"One would think," Henry echoed.

Johnson gave him a quizzical look but let the matter drop, for which Henry was grateful.

***

After returning home that evening, Hannah found Henry in the library.

"I thought your spirits might be too irritated to sleep," she said, leaning against the back of a chair as she watched him pace. "You really dislike Miss Dillinger, don't you?"

Henry shrugged. "It's not *her* that I dislike. It's..." Henry paused to find the right words. "There's a very specific type of lady Mother is pushing—firmly—in my direction."

Hannah nodded with a rueful smile. "I have noticed several similarities."

"And she and Father have made it quite clear that they think it my duty to marry one of those ladies for the sake of the duchy."

"So...?" Hannah seemed to be missing his point. "That's been true for years, and you've always refused. Why is it bothering you now?"

"They're nothing like Kate."

Hannah's expression darkened. "Henry Stanton, if you even think for a moment of throwing away your happiness and hers for some overblown notion of duty, I'll... I'll tell Mama about Kate."

It would have been a more worrisome threat if they'd still been in the country where Mother could pay a call at the tower and blow their secret.

"I'll tell her myself in the morning," Henry said, shaking his head. "I love Kate too much to give her up. But I'm worried how disappointed Mother will be. I don't want to upset her or

CHAPTER 14

cause a rift in the family. She has her heart set on me marrying an Incomparable."

"Only because she hasn't met Kate or seen the two of you together," Hannah argued. "Trust me, she just wants you to be happy and in love."

Henry wasn't as confident as his sister, but he let the debate drop and went to bed.

Mother cornered Henry in the library the next morning, where he'd just taken out his tool kit. His mind was too full of Kate and the impending confession to decide what to make next. He couldn't tolerate more dinners like Lord Haseltine's.

"You were not yourself last night," Mother said as she settled into a chair by the fire. "Lord and Lady Haseltine both commented on it. You barely spoke to either young lady at dinner."

Henry toyed with the bit of leather in his hands, waiting for his mother to finish saying her piece.

She traced the pattern of the brocade cushion with one finger, then sighed. When she spoke again, her voice was gentle. "I want to see you happily settled, Henry. How do you intend to find the right woman if you won't talk or dance?"

"I've already found Kate."

Mother's eyebrows shot up. She stared at him for a second before her mouth began to curve. "Who's Kate?" she asked innocently.

"Perfection," Henry murmured, thinking of her brilliant, artless smile and how her hand felt in his. "She's Hannah's friend."

"The mysterious friend she was visiting so often in the country?" Mother's smile broadened. "You've always been a most attentive brother, but I did wonder at how willingly you accompanied her on those visits. I'd assumed you were bored without Daniel at home."

"Not bored," Henry assured her. "Just in love."

"Why didn't you say something? We could have invited her to tea, or on a picnic..." Mother's eyes danced at the idea of Henry being in love, but her expression faltered when she noticed his. "Henry?"

"Her mother... doesn't approve of me."

She stiffened, her fingers gripping the arm of the chair. "Why, I've never heard of such a thing!"

Henry chuckled. "Never heard of a mother's disapproval?"

She gave him an unamused look. "Never heard of *anyone* disapproving of *you*."

Henry shook his head. "As far as she's concerned, no one is good enough for Kate."

"And what does Kate think?"

"I'm fairly confident Kate approves of me," he said, smiling.

"And you?"

"All I know is I want to give her everything she's ever dreamed of."

"*There's* the Henry I know and love." Mother smiled. "Very well. I will stop matchmaking, and I'll do my best to discourage the other mamas, but you really must dance occasionally. No more than one dance with each girl, naturally—no need to get anyone's hopes up—but at least be your usual, agreeable self."

Henry grinned, a weight lifted from his shoulders. "I'll do my best, Mother."

Chapter 15

Catherine felt in the gap of the split tree, her fingers brushing smooth paper. She grinned as she pulled it free, tucking her own into the gap in its place before hurrying back toward the tower. Mama's trips into the village had been short and sporadic ever since the Stantons had left so memorably for town. Catherine didn't dare linger outside the tower, let alone beyond the garden. She released the blue spell orb and climbed back into the kitchen window, vanishing the rope behind her. One quick glance to make sure she hadn't left a trace of her excursion, then she was hurrying up the stairs to her room.

She already had Hannah's letter unfolded by the time she collapsed onto her bed, tucking her feet up under her and laying the papers on the coverlet. Henry and his family had been gone for six weeks, and this was the sixth letter. All had been primarily from Hannah, though each had had a few lines added in Henry's hand, filling whatever space Hannah hadn't.

This week, Hannah described their visit to the theater. They'd seen *Pygmalion* before, and Hannah hadn't been impressed with this performance, though the orchestra was rather good. A friend of Henry's and another gentleman had stopped by at intermission. Henry's friend had left when the show recommenced, but the other gentleman, a Mr. Wilson, had stayed with them for the second act. "If you had been with us, Kate, there wouldn't have been an extra seat, and I would have been spared his attentions. Really, he is too dull for words. I missed you dreadfully then, and always, of course."

Catherine smiled at this. Hannah shared critiques of each suitor who called on her, and this was mild compared to some others. According to Hannah, the generality of London gentlemen were vain and self-centered, and all too often frequented gaming hells and other unsavory places.

"Henry, of course, is the exception," Hannah wrote. "He's so good and such a pleasant companion. All the old ladies dote on him. Several have tried to match him with any eligible relation. One countess tried to introduce him to her second cousin's niece. But while he's polite to all, his heart is untouchable."

Catherine wanted to take Hannah at her word, but she still held a lingering fear that Henry would forget her. His family—and by extension, he—had a very active social life, and he was more often than not in company with superior young ladies. How could Catherine hope to compare favorably? She had accomplishments, but she wouldn't fool herself into thinking she had poise or sophistication.

When Hannah's letter went on to describe their last evening at Almack's, a twist in her gut forced Catherine to stop reading. Hannah's letters were so full of detail about every event, and sometimes Catherine loved it—she loved picturing Hannah dressed up in fine gowns, enjoying herself at a grand assembly. But she hated it too. She hated feeling jealous of everyone who got to dance with Henry, who spoke to him, who received one of his knee-weakening smiles. She hated comparing herself to those unknown beauties. She hated that she was hiding in

CHAPTER 15

her room while they were experiencing life. She wanted to be there with them.

Catherine sighed and lay back on the bed. Yes, she wanted to be in London, but really, she'd gladly be anywhere but here. Whatever she'd told her friends in her letters, life in the tower had gone from stifling to smothering. She sometimes felt that she couldn't breathe without her mother's permission. Mama barely allowed her out of her sight. She could only walk in the garden in Mama's company, and her days were structured and supervised with a strict, new vigilance. If it weren't for the hope Henry gave her in each short message and for Hannah's unflinching friendship, she was afraid she'd implode under the pressure.

Could Mama not see that she was pushing Catherine away? Not that Catherine ever needed an excuse to think of Henry, but he filled her mind more than ever. Not only Henry but the family she'd been born into. She'd always wondered about who they were and what had happened to them, but now she considered ways to find answers. Asking Mama was pointless—the subject had long been forbidden, but Mama now rebuffed all questions, on nearly any subject, by giving her a new task to do or a sharp reprimand to focus on her work.

The best plan Catherine could come up with would be to go through the parish records for the month of her birth and see if there were any Catherines born who were not accounted for. This was hardly fail-proof. For all Catherine knew, she could have been born in a different parish, or perhaps she'd been given a different name by her birth mother. And how was she even to get to the magistrate's office to look through the records when she couldn't leave the tower? She confided all of this to Hannah and Henry, pouring out her ponderings into letters. They couldn't help from town, but it was a relief to talk to someone about it.

Catherine waited for the jealousy to subside before sitting up and finishing reading the letter. Hannah had left a few inches at the bottom for Henry. Driving his sisters through Hyde Park again, he'd noticed the daffodils and tulips and how green the grass looked after last week's rain. It was the perfect scene for a watercolor. "I can't think of many things I want more than to sit with you while you paint it," he wrote. "But one is to see you again and say hello in the same way I said goodbye."

Catherine blushed. She wanted another kiss too. She reread Henry's words until she'd committed them to memory, then she took the pages to the empty hearth. A whispered spell-word sent the paper up in flames. Shriveled, blackened, and finally ash. Catherine used another spell to waft it up and out the window to catch the spring breeze that blew through the trees, leaving no trace in her room of any contact with the outside world.

***

Nine. The number reverberated in Henry's head as he dressed for another private ball. Nine weeks in town. Nine weeks away from Kate. Nine weeks of balls and assemblies and card parties and dinners. Nine weeks of being agreeable to people he'd rather avoid—well, more like six, if one asked Mother, because he'd been less than charming for the first few weeks here.

He was ready to return to Cauldercrest. Spring was well underway, and he missed the scent of rain on the new grass. The fog and drizzle of London oppressed without refreshing.

CHAPTER 15

Hannah was wearying of town as well, he could see. She'd been eager before each event for the first few weeks, but lately she'd seemed more resigned, stoic. She went because that was what one did, not because she expected any benefit from it.

Henry sighed. His sister was too young to be jaded by the *ton* already.

Tonight's ball, hosted by Lady Sterling, was less of a crush than some others, but still crowded enough to show just how popular the lady was. Her ballroom was larger and grander than some, so perhaps she simply had more room to fit everyone. Hannah cast her eyes around the crowd.

"Searching for someone?" Henry asked, leaning closer.

"Don't be silly," Hannah said, standing on tiptoe for a moment to see above a lady's head. "Who would I want to see that I haven't seen a dozen times over?"

"Excellent question." Henry smothered a grin. "Perhaps you're only hoping for a good dancer for a first partner."

Hannah made a noncommittal noise.

Henry stayed by his sister's side until her dance card was full and her first partner claimed her. It was Mr. Wilson, the second son of the Marquess of Gladwell, and from Hannah's politely blank expression, he was *not* the person she'd been looking for. Henry set off to dance himself then. He avoided the acknowledged beauties, and Miss Dillinger in particular. They had beaux in spades, and they believed they deserved every ounce of the attention. Their consequence didn't need to be puffed up any more by a dance with a duke's heir. Instead, he made a point to ask the ladies on the fringes: the plain girls, the ones who had been out for several seasons, the wallflowers. One dance with each, but one was enough—enough to draw the notice of other gentlemen to the lady, enough to keep Henry unavailable to dance with the Incomparables with scheming mamas.

He sat out a dance midway through the evening. With a glass of punch in hand, he looked for Hannah to see how she fared. She was partnered with Johnson, the usually graceless dancer who looked remarkably surefooted at the moment. Hannah's eyes sparkled as she laughed at something he said. Henry smiled and turned away.

His gaze landed on someone so familiar he nearly dropped his cup. His breath caught, and his heart thudded in his chest. He stared for a long moment before what he was seeing registered in his brain. It *wasn't* Kate. This woman was older, her hair a deeper wheaten shade, though the curls that escaped the pins gave her the same sort of halo in the candlelight. She'd be about the same height as Kate, and her eyes, as she chatted with the lady beside her, shone the same cornflower blue.

Henry hardly dared take his eyes off her as he found his mother in the crowd. Drawing her aside, he asked if she knew the woman.

"The one in the deep blue dress and sapphires?" Mother asked. "That's Lady Rampion, dear. Why?"

"She looks just like Kate."

"I expect Kate looks like *her*—Lady Rampion's my age."

Mother was probably more accurate than she knew, if Henry's guess about the woman's relation to the girl was correct.

"How well do you know her?"

"Well enough. We came out the same season and have attended many of the same events over the years." Mother looked at him suspiciously. "What are you thinking of?"

"I've had an idea that I need your help with," Henry said, still studying Lady Rampion. "But first, there's something I haven't told you about Kate..."

***

Henry was in the library later that night when the door opened and Hannah entered. The firelight made her nightdress and shawl glow rosily. Henry set aside the decorative leather harness he was working on, laying it on the table beside his now tepid tea.

"Couldn't sleep?" he asked, glancing at the clock on the mantle as Hannah took a seat in the brocade armchair across from him. Two o'clock in the morning.

She shook her head "Too much excitement. It always takes me a while to fall asleep after a ball, but tonight's worse. I was hoping to find a really dull book."

Henry waved a hand at the shelves. "Take your pick." He stood and went to the sideboard. "Ratafia?"

"Please."

He poured two small glasses of the mild liqueur. Neither of them liked stronger drinks, but Hannah could use some help winding down. He handed her the glass, and she drank it slowly. Henry took a sip of his own and set the glass on the table. He sat back down.

"You're up late," Hannah said at last.

"I miss Kate."

She smiled. "I miss her too. Only a few more weeks." She studied the liquid in her glass. "Do you think she's telling the whole truth about how things are with her mother?"

"No." Henry frowned. There had been an underlying current of discontent in her letters that had grown stronger with the passing weeks. Half to himself, he murmured, "I should have carried her off to Scotland months ago."

"I told you to," Hannah agreed.

"She deserves better," he said, giving his sister the same argument he'd made with himself over and over. "She deserves a proper wedding with friends and family present."

"*We're* her friends, and her only family doesn't like you," Hannah pointed out. "I'll come along to stand with her, if you like, and be chaperone until you reach Gretna Green. We could even take the trip as a family." She giggled at the idea. "I don't think anyone's ever taken their whole family when eloping before."

Henry rolled his eyes. "Probably not, but it's not the worst idea you've had."

"Of course it's not. My ideas are always good." She swallowed the last of her ratafia and grinned at him. "I'm a delight, and you love me."

"All true," Henry chuckled. "On a different topic, now that we've settled my life, I noticed you dancing with Johnson tonight. Any broken toes?"

He couldn't tell if Hannah's cheeks pinked or if it was the firelight. Her smile softened slightly, and she said, "His dancing has improved this season."

"With you, perhaps. I saw him trip twice while dancing with Miss Dillinger."

She looked offended at his grin. "You oughtn't laugh at your friend's discomfiture."

His grin only widened. "Not his. *Hers.*"

Hannah's eyes twinkled, and she couldn't hide her amusement. Not that either of them would wish Johnson involved, but neither could regret an Incomparable suffering through a

CHAPTER 15

dance with a graceless partner.

After a moment, Hannah said, "You've been doing a good thing, you know, dancing with the nobodies."

Henry nodded, his good mood sinking again. The conversation had circled back around to him missing Kate. He'd made the best of the situation he'd been given, but he'd rather dance with Kate than anyone in the world.

Hannah went up to bed soon after, taking a book from a shelf at random. The clock struck three. Henry still had no hope of sleep, but he couldn't concentrate on anything else, either. He worried about Kate, about what new restrictions her mother had put in place. He worried about the depressed spirits he'd detected in her letters. When dawn lightened the sky through the windows to a dull gray, he went to the stables, quietly saddling one of the carriage horses without waking anyone. He led the horse to the street before mounting. It went with him willingly, having been through several such early rides over the past weeks. Galloping alone through Hyde Park in the misty morning hours was the only thing that kept him from galloping into the country to rescue Kate. Restraining himself had grown harder and harder, but he had a new plan to implement with Mother, and he couldn't leave before it was underway. So a morning ride would have to do.

The sun was up and climbing, though the hour was still well before breakfast, when Henry headed back for Berkeley Square. A friendly voice hailed him, and he reined in his horse, turning to look. Johnson walked along an adjoining path, still in his evening attire. Henry had at least changed when he'd gotten home after the ball, though it looked like Johnson hadn't been home at all.

"What are you doing out at this hour?"

"I could ask you the same," Johnson said.

"It's the only time I can go for a proper ride. Clears my head." Henry shrugged and dismounted, leading his horse so he could fall into step beside his friend. "And you?"

"Wortle and I went for a drink after the ball. He got a trifle foxed, so I saw him home, and he insisted on a game of cards." Johnson stuck his hands in his pockets. "Neither of us bet anything—wouldn't have been sporting to take advantage of him in that condition. And now I'm headed home to sleep."

They fell silent, watching a street sweeper brush the paving stones down the way.

"What's going on with you?" Johnson asked after a while, shooting Henry a look. "You're not yourself this year."

"How so? I'm being perfectly agreeable, and my sister commended my choice of dance partners."

"Far be it from me to disagree with Lady Hannah." Johnson's mouth quirked at the corners. "I doubt most of the *ton* would notice. I just know you better. You're more reserved than usual. And I'm not just talking about that absurd dinner party where you spoke to no one. It's any time you're in company beyond your family. Add in the unprecedentedly early rides—I know this isn't your first ride of the Season, but it's definitely the first Season you've done it…. It's like you're restless and itching to be anywhere but here."

Henry wouldn't meet his friend's eyes. "Not quite *any*where."

"Talk, man. I'm your best mate."

Johnson had a point. Henry really should have told him weeks ago. "I met someone this summer."

"Ah." Johnson drew out the sound. "Someone female who lives in the vicinity of Cauldercrest, I take it. Someone beside whom everyone else pales in comparison?"

CHAPTER 15

"Precisely."

Johnson nodded as if that explained it all. They'd reached the end of the drive, and Henry paused. "I wasn't trying to keep it from you. Habitual secret, you see. I only just told Mother about her after that disastrous dinner party."

"Perfectly understandable," Johnson said, smothering a yawn. "I'm off to bed, but I'll see you tomorrow, and I expect you to tell me everything."

"Come for dinner. Mother's been bemoaning how long it's been since you've been round."

They nodded farewell, and Henry led the horse back to the stable where a groom was awake and waiting to care for it. Henry removed his boots just inside the door and took the stairs silently to his room so as not to disturb the rest of his family. Exhaustion caught up to him, and he fell into bed without doing more than removing his coat and cravat.

Chapter 16

Catherine perused the bookshelves in the library, not looking for anything in particular. She couldn't sit still to play the harp, and she couldn't hide her restlessness from Mama, who was preparing a tray of buns to bake for dinner. So Catherine had chosen the library for her refuge. She paced the small circular room. Hannah's last letter, dated from London over two weeks ago, had declared that they'd be leaving town in a fortnight. Which meant that the family was settled in Cauldercrest by now.

Butterflies swirled in Catherine's stomach. She'd see Henry soon, maybe even today. Mama hadn't been to the village in a full week, and they were running low on butter and eggs, and Mama had used the last of the flour mixing up the dough for the buns. If Catherine could predict her mother—a skill she'd perfected over the years, though Mama's increasingly erratic and irrational behavior made the task more difficult—Mama would go to the village while the buns were rising.

Catherine would put the shawl in the window as soon as Mama was out of sight, but would Henry see it? Mama's trips to the village were so unpredictable that she hadn't been able to tell him what day to expect when she'd written last. Would he come today? Or had he come yesterday and she'd missed

CHAPTER 16

him?

She put a hand to her stomach as the butterflies swooped sickeningly. Why did falling in love have to be so complicated?

"Kitty," Mama called up from the kitchen.

Whether from the shape of the tower or a spell Mama had cast on it, Catherine didn't know, but sound carried exceptionally well from floor to floor. It meant that Mama could hear her practicing the harp in her room no matter what room Mama was in. It also meant that they didn't have to continually climb stairs to speak to each other, nor did they have to raise their voices above what was ladylike.

"In the library, Mama," Catherine called back.

"I'm going to the village. I'll be back by the time the buns are ready."

"Yes, Mama."

"What will you be doing?"

"I'm just looking for a book I haven't read yet." It was true, in its way—that was what her eyes were scanning the shelves for. But it was only a small part of the truth. Catherine's stomach knotted at the knowledge that she'd become uncomfortably adept at lying to her mother by omission.

"I'll see if I can find something new at the lending library."

That small kindness made Catherine feel even worse. Yes, her mother was overbearing and controlling and irrationally overprotective, but she still loved Catherine more than anything. If only she'd loosen her grip a bit.

Catherine stood at the window and watched her mother cross the garden, her face hidden behind her bonnet. Catherine frowned as the familiar pause at the wall stretched longer than usual. Had Mama changed the boundary spell? But then Mama was gone between the trees, and Catherine hurried up to her room to hang her shawl.

She skipped down the steps two at a time, leaving her bonnet and gloves on the shelf as she conjured her golden rope and climbed out the window. It was a beautiful May day, warm and sunny, too fine to be cooped up indoors. The air smelled fresh and green after yesterday's rain. Catherine sucked in deep breaths as she walked the garden paths, trying not to let herself glance at the woods too often and disappointed each time she failed and saw no one.

She gave the vegetable garden a wide berth: Mama would notice if Catherine had been working there, and she'd know that she'd left the tower. But there was no harm in enjoying the lilacs or the tulips. Catherine bent occasionally to pluck a weed, but mostly she simply soaked in the colors and fragrance, pretending that the butterflies in her stomach weren't multiplying the longer she waited.

And then she heard it, from across the garden, the voice she'd ached to hear for months. "Kate?"

She straightened, turned. He stood just beyond the garden wall, his hat in his hands. The breeze ruffled his brown hair. Every plane of his face was familiar and precious. Catherine stood staring, unable to move. The butterflies calmed as she held Henry's gaze. He was here. He'd come back.

He moved to take a step forward, and suddenly Catherine's feet were free of their spell. She ran to meet him, ready to fling her arms around his neck and never let go. But her steps faltered. He hadn't entered the garden. He wasn't coming to her with the same joy. His expression held no joy at all, only confusion as he frowned down at the low wall.

He looked up and met her eyes as she slowed to a stop within the barrier. "I can't come through."

CHAPTER 16

"What? Why not?"

Henry put out a hand and pushed against the air between them. Nothing happened.

"She must have added to the boundary spell after you left." Catherine spoke the spell-word to remove the spell, settling the ball of magic between two gone-by daffodils. "Can you come through now?"

But Henry was already beside her, pulling her close and crushing his lips against hers. This kiss held less of the sweetness and longing of the first. It was hungry and desperate, a filling of emptiness. Catherine clung to him, responding with the same craving. When they came up for air, Catherine's head was spinning. Henry rested his forehead against hers.

"I've come every day since we got back," he breathed. "Being away from you has been torture."

Catherine nodded. She couldn't string two words together yet.

"Has it been awful for you here?"

She nodded again, unable to hide from him how oppressive she'd found the new rules. "I'd have gone mad if not for the letters," she said. "But then, sometimes I thought the letters would send me mad instead."

"Did they make it worse?" Henry pulled back to search her eyes. "I was afraid if Hannah told you what you were missing—"

Catherine shook her head. "It wasn't that. It was…" She bit her lip, and her next words were barely a whisper. "I was jealous of everyone who danced with you." She looked at her feet.

Henry lifted her chin. "I didn't want to dance with them. I only wanted to dance with you. I hated every assembly because you weren't there."

She watched the gold flicker in the green and brown of his eyes. They were distracting, and she heard her own voice as if from a distance say, "Hannah told me that you always asked the outcasts on the fringes of the *ton*."

Henry nodded. "I could do a kindness without raising any expectations."

Catherine blinked, trying to shake her mind free. "Are you doing a kindness with me? I'm not even on the fringes of society. Am *I* a good deed? Is it... does it bother you if I have hopes, if not expectations?"

"I want nothing more than for you to have expectations." Henry's breath tickled her ear as he leaned in. "I want to meet your expectations, exceed your wildest hopes. You've never been a good deed. You make me want to be better. Can you not see that yet? Have I not made myself clear enough?"

He slipped his arms around her. Catherine leaned her head against his collarbone, and he kissed her hair.

"You're *every*thing, Kate."

His arms were strong and warm, and Catherine felt at home in a way she'd never felt before. She'd always thought that home was the tower, but now she understood: home was a person. *This* person. This one person who saw her and knew her and put her needs and dreams first.

She raised her head, and they kissed again, a kiss full of promises.

Catherine pulled back with a gasp. "How long have we been out here? Mama will be home any minute."

"When can I take you away from here?" he asked. "When can we stop hiding?"

"Soon." She stood on tiptoe and kissed his cheek. "But I'm afraid of what she'll do—she's been acting so strangely lately."

CHAPTER 16

"Do you think she'll curse us?"

Catherine recoiled at the idea, but she couldn't deny it with the vehemence she wished for. "I... don't know. I think she loves me too much to curse me, but..." Lately, Mama had been unpredictable, and Catherine knew she was a magician of some power. "We just need to make a plan."

Henry nodded, obviously still concerned but willing to trust her judgment. "I'll be back every day next week."

Her heart soared knowing that he wouldn't miss his chance to see her, no matter when it came.

With Henry back on the other side of the wall, Catherine released the spell. She watched him jog into the tree shadows to one side just as another figure emerged from the path.

Catherine's heart stuttered and flopped to her feet as her mother scowled. "What are you doing outside?" Mama snapped as she approached.

"It was such a beautiful day," Catherine squeaked. "I wanted fresh air."

"You could have waited half an hour for me."

Mama stalked through the boundary spell and up to Catherine. For such a slight person, she seemed to loom menacingly. Catherine saw the moment the scowl of irritation morphed into a glower of rage. Mama's dark eyes flashed behind her spectacles, and Catherine struggled not to cower.

"You promised," Mama hissed, "that it would never happen again."

Catherine's eyes went wide, and she couldn't breathe. The kisses. How stupid could she be, to forget that Mama would know? She'd been too caught up in Henry to think clearly. What had she done?

"How could you do this to me?" Mama demanded, chill and

sharp and acerbic. "After all I've done for you, all I've done to protect you, you *lied* to me? You threw yourself at some stranger like a Cyprian? Like a common light-skirt?"

A sick, acidic burning filled Catherine's stomach, more nauseating by far than the swooping nerves she'd felt earlier. She *had* lied, and she *had* kissed Henry, but her mother's harsh accusations cut cruelly. She opened her mouth to protest, but her mother grabbed her elbow and towed her to the house, her iron grip implacable. Mama's nostrils flared at the sight of Catherine's golden rope, but she didn't speak. The semi-visible stairs appeared in response to a silent spell, and she hauled Catherine up these as well. Not a word was spoken in the kitchen or the entire way up staircase after staircase to Catherine's room. Mama released her arm with a slight shove that sent her falling onto the edge of her bed. Catherine rubbed at where her mother's fingers had left white marks on her skin.

"How did he even get in? Or did *you* get *out*?" Mama's eyes were wide and wild. "I cannot believe you would go behind my back like this," she fumed. "Secrets and lies and liaisons—I *trusted* you!"

Catherine could have argued that banning her from social interactions and confining her to the tower hardly constituted trust. Instead she said, "He loves me, Mama. He wants to marry me. He's the son of a duke—he'll take good care of me."

Mama's eyes narrowed. "Has he proposed?"

Catherine hesitated. "Not quite."

"Has he told you outright that he loves you?"

Again, Catherine's mouth worked before she forced herself to say, "Not in so many words."

"You see? Obstinate, foolish girl! Men are not to be trusted, and clearly you cannot be trusted either. You will remain in

CHAPTER 16

your room until you prove to me that you have learned from your mistakes."

Mama turned on her heel and descended the stairs, leaving Catherine alone and shaken. How had her day gone from so wonderful to so horrible, and so quickly? Why hadn't she run off with Henry this morning when she had the chance?

Chapter 17

Henry was walking on air for the next two days. A weight had lifted from his chest; he could breathe again. His smile felt more genuine than it had in months. Hannah noticed—he caught her smirking at him several times, but she had the good grace not to comment.

The next week, he did what he'd promised: he rode to the woods near the tower every morning and checked the topmost window for a flash of bright blue. If Kate wanted a plan for escaping her mother, they would make one. He could have Hannah ready to leave with them for Scotland within the week. He could hire a magician to protect them from spells designed to find Kate and drag her back. They were so close to making a life together, and Henry wouldn't let anything get in the way.

On Thursday, he got his sign. The sky-blue shawl hung in Kate's window. He left Honey tethered just within the trees and approached the garden wall. The barrier still prevented him from passing through.

"Kate!"

There she was in her window. She waved. He pushed against the air with one hand. A sudden rush of wind caused him to stumble back. It vanished as quickly as it came, and Henry reached for the barrier again. It was gone. He passed through

CHAPTER 17

and approached the tower. "Kate?" he called again.

"Henry!" Kate's voice sounded muffled and echoed strangely, as though it wasn't coming from her window on the far side of the tower. He couldn't pinpoint where it was coming from. "Climb up! I need your help—something's wrong."

One of Kate's magical ropes hung from the kitchen window, and Henry didn't hesitate to haul himself up. He clambered into the kitchen and straightened, finding himself face to face with a short woman with her dark hair pulled severely back, her dark eyes flashing ferociously.

"You," she snarled.

***

Catherine had watched her mother leave and check the boundary spell before hanging the shawl. She sat by her window to wait, unmoving. She'd spent most of the last week just sitting. A kind of lethargy had fallen on her after Mama had sent her to her room. The stairs to the lower levels had been blocked by a spell, but there was no point in removing it. There was no reason to increase Mama's ire, and Catherine was too tired anyway. Her brain felt slow and foggy, and the air felt as thick and heavy as treacle.

Henry's shout woke her from her stupor, and she waved. He pushed against the boundary, and she realized that she'd forgotten about Mama's additions. Could she remove it from here? She put all of her currently limited powers of concentration into the spell and spoke the word. With a rush, a blue orb of power appeared above her hand. She set it gently on her pillow. Looking at her hairbrush on her vanity, she decided it would take her too long to wade across the room.

Why was she so slow and tired? This wasn't right. Shaking her head to clear it, she tugged a few golden strands that had escaped her braid and spoke the spell to turn them into rope. Slowly, thickly, she secured the end and dropped the rope out the window.

"Climb up!" she called, leaning against the window frame, eyes closed. "I need your help—something's wrong."

She waited for Henry's weight to shift the rope, but nothing happened. Catherine opened her eyes and peered out. Where was he? Why did everything feel so unnatural and off-kilter?

Catherine held out her hand, palm up, like she did to take down the boundary spell and spoke the spell again, trying to remove the fog in her brain, but nothing happened. She said it again, concentrating on the thick, cloying air in the room, but still nothing. Harborough's spell wouldn't work if she didn't know what magic she was undoing. A vague sense of wrongness was evidently not enough.

Voices from below froze her where she stood, her blood turning to ice in her veins. Her breath caught, her heart stuttered, and a chill ran down her spine. Mama was supposed to be in the village. She'd watched her leave. What was she doing here? Was this... a trap?

***

Henry backed up until he was pressed against the windowsill.

"You," Miss Whitmer said again, prowling slowly forward. "You have a lot of nerve climbing into my house."

"Forgive me, ma'am," Henry said. "I am Lord Henry Stanton, and—"

"I don't care who you are! I want you to get out and leave me

CHAPTER 17

and my daughter alone!"

"I'll go, but, please, I love your daughter more than life itself. Is she all right?"

She narrowed a glare at him. "She's fine, no thanks to you. You've *ruined* her."

Henry stiffened. "I've done nothing of the sort, and I'll marry her today if you'll just let me *see* her—"

"Never!" The snarl sounded more like a wild animal than ever. "You won't take my daughter from me. I won't lose her. Not to you, not to anyone!"

Henry held his hands in front of him, placating. "Please," he said, as calmly and softly as he could, though his heart was thundering, "please, may I just see Kate?"

"Her name is not Kate!" Miss Whitmer screeched. "You have no right to address her so informally! And you will never see her again—I am her mother, and I won't allow it!"

She flew at him, and Henry scrambled out the window and down the rope, dropping heavily to the ground as Kate's unhinged mother shrieked a nonsense word after him. He turned to hurry back through the garden, deciding that he needed to hire a magician *now*, but he stumbled, his vision suddenly blurring, graying, fading, until everything was white. He couldn't see the garden, he couldn't see the tower, he couldn't see the spinster magician calling hurtful names at him from the window. Her voice at least gave him a sense of which way to go to get away. He stumbled and tripped over a bush, and then into a bench, weaving blindly through the garden and probably trampling half of it.

***

Catherine heard every word of the conversation thanks to the magically augmented acoustics of the tower.

I love your daughter more than life itself.

Henry's words launched her heart skywards, and she tried again and again to undo the spell she was under to no avail. When her mother started screaming at him, Catherine gave up on magic. She squeezed her eyes shut tight and climbed out the window, pretending it was only the short drop from the kitchen and not the full height of the tower. She slid down the rope so fast it burned her hands, but she didn't care. A fresh breeze blew around her, clearing her head as if blowing away the fog. Her feet hit the ground hard, and she propped one arm against the wall to steady herself as she took a deep breath. Then she picked up her skirts and dashed around the tower.

Henry was stumbling away, crashing through flower beds. He knocked over the birdbath. Catherine called his name, and he paused, lifting his head and turning slightly toward her. She gasped. His eyes, clouded by a milky film, stared at her, unseeing. Her chest ached, and a lump formed in her throat. This was not how today was supposed to go.

"Kitty, what do you think you're doing? Get back here right now!"

Catherine whirled on her mother, who was standing in the kitchen window, prepared to come down.

"No," she snapped. "Enough is enough. I can't take another minute. How could you possibly think that this—" she gestured at Henry—"*any* of this—" she waved broadly to encompass the tower and garden—"is acceptable behavior? You locked me in my room, you put a *spell* on me, you blinded Henry! You've gone too far." Tears leaked down her cheeks as Catherine glared at her mother. "You always say that you don't want to lose me,

CHAPTER 17

but you've done nothing but push me away for months. I love you—you know I do—but this is intolerable."

Mama gaped, dumbfounded. Catherine spun on her heel and strode to Henry, slipping her arm through his and leading him as quickly as she dared through the garden.

Just as they reached the wall, Mama found her voice, a deranged screech. "If you set foot out of this garden, I will never see you again, you ungrateful wretch!"

Catherine paused, prepared to shout another long-deserved caustic retort, but the sadness that flooded her choked out the words. Mama may mean to hurt her, but she wouldn't respond in kind. She'd said her piece, and now her actions could speak for themselves.

She led Henry from the garden to where Honey whinnied at them from the edge of the woods. She untied the horse and led him by the reins in her free hand as she guided Henry with the other.

They didn't stop until they reached the lightning-split tree, well out of sight of the tower. Then Catherine turned to Henry. He blinked at her blindly.

"I'm so sorry," she whispered, weeping again. "I should have gone with you last week. I should have known she'd find out. It's all my fault."

"No, Kate. You're not responsible for her actions."

"Maybe not, but—"

"What's done is done," he said gently.

Catherine reached up and took his face in her hands, gently using her thumbs to close his eyes and pulling him down so that she could press a kiss to each eyelid. She whispered the spell-word, focusing easily on the very concrete problem, and a small blue orb appeared at her shoulder. Letting go of Henry, she placed the orb in the hollow of the tree.

When she looked back at Henry, she was caught by the blend of brown and green and gold, a surprising amount of gold, in his eyes.

"Did you mean what you said to her?" she asked softly.

"That I'd marry you today? Absolutely."

"And that you love me?"

"With all my heart." He took her hands and tugged her closer. "I love you, Kate."

"I love you too," she breathed.

"And you'll marry me?"

Catherine stood on tiptoe and pressed a light kiss to his lips. "Of course I will."

He pulled her in for a more thorough kiss, but even that was short because the shadow of the tower was not the place for dallying. Henry mounted Honey, and, like Catherine's very first ride, he helped her up to sit in front of him. She still felt shaken by the events of the morning, and emotions raged within her, but Henry's arms held her securely, giving her peace amid the storm.

Chapter 18

Henry's description of his family home did not prepare Catherine at all for her first sight of Cauldercrest. Intellectually, she knew it was a grand, sprawling stone house situated in a large park with a lake. But years had passed since she'd been in any building besides her tower, which consisted of six single-room floors. She couldn't even guess at how many rooms were side by side on each floor of the rambling mansion. She gaped at it, her eyes practically popping out of her head as she tried to take it all in.

"What do you think?" Henry murmured in her ear as he reined Honey to a stop in the courtyard before the door.

A groom hurried to take the horse's head, and Henry dismounted then lifted Catherine down. He was watching her, waiting, but she couldn't find words. She shook her head, hoping that he could tell that she was overcome and not disapproving. He smiled, and she smiled back, feeling again that surety that *Henry* was her home, and as long as he was comfortable here, she could be too.

The front door flung open as they approached, and Hannah ushered them inside

"I've missed you!" She embraced Catherine tightly. "Mama will be here momentarily. Mary saw you ride up, so it wasn't long before the whole house heard." She shook her head at her younger sister's antics. Hannah took Catherine's hand and squeezed it. "Are you well, Kate?"

Catherine took a breath, about to assure her friend that she was fine, but she let it out as a long sigh instead. "I don't rightly know," she said. "I'm not hurt, but I confess I'm rather shaken."

Hannah put an arm around her shoulders, and Henry took her free hand and held it. Their mother found them like this a moment later when she bustled into the entrance hall.

"From the hubbub your sister was making you'd think she'd never seen Henry ride a horse before." She gestured in exasperation, before giving Catherine a warm smile. "Hello, dear. Welcome. Am I to guess that you're Hannah's friend Kate?"

Catherine curtsied as best she could with her friends still holding on to her. "I am, Your Grace. Please forgive me for intruding so suddenly."

The duchess cut her off with a wave. "Not at all, dear, you're not intruding. I've heard so much about you from both Hannah and Henry, and I'm delighted to finally meet you. Have you come to visit for the day?"

"Actually, Mother, there's been... an altercation of sorts..." Henry began, glancing at Catherine.

"I can't go back," she said quietly. "I *won't* go back."

Her Grace let out a little *oh* of surprise and sympathy, but the warmth never left her eyes. "You're welcome to stay here with us. I'm sure we can find clothes to fit you among Hannah's and Mary's things. We'll put you in the rooms right next to Hannah's."

"Thank you, ma'am."

"Call me Alice, dear. You're practically family."

CHAPTER 18

"Does this mean we're off to Gretna Green?" Hannah asked eagerly.

Catherine blushed. She and Henry hadn't had a chance to talk about running away together, but it seemed Hannah knew what was coming and was prepared to come along as chaperone until the wedding could take place.

The duchess scoffed. "I'm sure there's no call to be going so far as Scotland."

Hannah turned curious eyes on her mother. "Do you think Daniel will consent to do it?"

Catherine had forgotten that Henry's brother was a clergyman. "Even though I'm underage without parental permission?"

The duchess—Alice—patted Catherine's arm. "We'll talk to him," she said. "For now, let's get you settled in. I'm sure you'd like to rest after your eventful morning."

Henry gave Catherine's hand a final squeeze and relinquished her to Hannah's care with a reassuring smile. Hannah linked arms with her and led her up the enormous staircase to the wing where their rooms awaited. Catherine was beginning to feel somewhat numb. Everything in the house was made of stone and polished wood and rich fabrics. Each room was so *big*, and there was furniture everywhere. There were people everywhere, too, servants going about their business and shooting curious glances their way. Mary appeared at the door of her room across the hall from Hannah's to give Catherine a bright smile.

"Are you staying?" she asked brightly. Mary's hair was a lighter honey brown than Hannah's, and her eyes were more green, but otherwise the sisters looked very much alike. "I'm in the middle of lessons, but I couldn't have borne missing your visit entirely. They finally told me about you just weeks ago—to think they kept you a secret all this time!" With a little wave, she disappeared back through the doorway.

Catherine blinked after her. She never would have called Hannah reserved, but now she could see that the elder sister was nothing compared to the younger.

"You'll get used to her," Hannah said, tugging Catherine to an open door a little farther down the hall. "She's great fun most of the time. But don't entrust her with secrets. She can't keep one to save her life."

A middle-aged woman with neat silvering-blonde hair and a perfectly pressed dress and apron bustled about inside the room Hannah led her to. The room itself was twice the size of Catherine's tower room, with a wardrobe, a vanity, a washstand, three chairs, and a small bookshelf, all in the same pale wood with lavender upholstery and cream ribbons. Through another open door to one side, Catherine could see a big fourposter bed spread with a matching lavender-and-cream counterpane. It was a room for a princess, not a magician's runaway daughter. Catherine stood stunned.

"Are you the famous Kate, then?" the woman asked.

Catherine nodded mutely.

"This is Mrs. Knight, our beloved housekeeper," Hannah said, beaming at the woman.

"Oh," Catherine said, finding her voice at last. "The letters—thank you."

Mrs. Knight smiled broadly, her eyes crinkling at the corners. "I've always wanted to take part in a clandestine, well, *anything*, so it was my pleasure, I assure you." She passed the girls on her way to the door, then turned back. "Lady Hannah, I'll begin going through your wardrobe. Let me know if you need

CHAPTER 18

anything."

"Thank you. I'll be right there."

Mrs. Knight left, and Hannah led an unresisting Catherine to the nearest chair. She pushed her gently into it, then sank into the next one herself.

"Make yourself at home, Kate. I won't pester you for details of what happened this morning, but know that I'm here to talk whenever or if ever you're ready." She smiled wryly as she gazed around the room. "Not that I've ever been inside your tower, but I'd imagine this is all quite an adjustment, so take your time. I'll let you rest while I go see about some clothes for you, and I'll come back to get you for dinner." She stood and moved toward the door.

"Corners," Catherine said, leaning her head back against the chair. She glanced up at her friend, who was frowning in confusion. She laughed. "There are so many things that you'd think would be stranger to adjust to, but I've never been in a room with corners before."

Hannah grinned. "And I can't imagine a room without them." She slipped out the door.

Catherine swept the room with one more look, then closed her eyes. The past several hours had been so overwhelming that she just wanted to shut it all out for a while. Not that she could shut out her memories, the voices in her mind. Her mother's voice, harsh and hurtful. Henry's voice, declaring that he loved her more than life itself. Her own voice, telling her mother that such behavior would no longer be tolerated and that she couldn't stay a moment longer.

Catherine groaned. Mama had been shocked speechless by her tirade. Could she not see it coming? Could she have deluded herself so severely? Or had she seen it and fought against it so hard that she achieved the exact thing she'd been trying to prevent?

A sigh escaped, taking with it a load of tension she'd been carrying so long she'd forgotten it existed and replacing it with relief. Most spells required the magician to be within sight for the casting, so if Mama was still angry enough to want to curse her, she'd have to come to Cauldercrest. After her last threat, disowning Catherine, it was unlikely she'd take that path. Even if she tried, Catherine knew Henry would use his impressive household staff to keep her mother out. If Mama tried anything on any of them, the magistrates would be called down on her head in moments. No, Mama could not curse her or drag her back to the tower. Catherine was safe here, among friends.

But the broken place in her life where Mama and her tower home had been ripped out—albeit by her own hand—was still jagged and sore.

***

Catherine and Hannah were walking in the garden when a servant requested their presence in the drawing room to receive guests. Catherine had been staying at Cauldercrest for four days. She was still wearing borrowed gowns, which were about the right size though several inches too short. Mary's solution had been to present her with a dizzying array of lace from her collection, and between the three of them, the girls had sewn on the trim to extend the hems. Catherine already loved Henry's family and felt an unfamiliar but wonderful sense of belonging with them. Nothing more had been said about Scotland. Hannah had asked at dinner the third night

CHAPTER 18

if her mother had heard from Daniel, and she'd replied that she hadn't had a letter from him, though she didn't expect one for another day or two yet. The duchess had exchanged a look with Henry then, and Catherine had felt a kind of tension pass between them, expectation or perhaps anticipation. What did they know that they weren't saying?

They could hear the duchess in the drawing room as they drew near, and Henry was talking as well. Catherine followed Hannah into the room, nervous of meeting more strangers. To her relief, there were only two people in the room besides Henry's family. Henry spoke to a boy a year or two younger than Catherine, just at the age between boyhood and manhood, tallish and blond and eager. A woman who must be the boy's mother sat with Alice on a settee. She had dark golden curls that escaped their elegant knot and vibrant blue eyes. She looked up at the girls as they entered, and when her gaze fell on Catherine, she went ashen. Catherine, too, felt stunned, frozen in place. She'd never seen this woman before, but she knew her. Tearing her eyes away, she glanced around the room. The boy who'd been talking to Henry was looking back and forth between Catherine and his mother, and even Hannah darted looks between the two. Henry and his mother wore matching satisfied smiles.

"I say," the boy said. "What's going on here? Who're you?"

"Where are my manners?" Alice beamed. "My daughter, Lady Hannah Stanton, and her friend, Miss Catherine Whitmer."

"Catherine... Whitmer...?"

"Just Kate, please," Catherine said quietly.

The woman, if possible, grew paler.

"And may I present Lady Rampion and her son, Lucas Templeton?"

Curtsies and bows followed, then Catherine studied Lucas as he openly examined her. He looked strikingly familiar, though she couldn't for the life of her understand why. She looked at Henry, perplexed, but it was Hannah who repeated Lucas's question.

"What's going on?"

"Mother introduced me to Lady Rampion in town," Henry said, his eyes on Catherine. "Kate had told us that she was adopted, and she'd been curious about the family she was born to." He glanced at the obviously shaken lady whose hand his mother was now holding. "We thought you all ought to meet each other."

Lucas rounded on his mother. "I have a sister? Why didn't you tell me?"

Lady Rampion nodded weakly. "All the parish records say that our daughter Catherine died on her first birthday. I knew it for a lie, but the truth was too complicated, so we didn't speak of it."

Catherine took an involuntary step forward. "What *is* the truth?"

Lady Rampion opened her mouth, closed it, and shook her head.

"Hannah, why don't you and Kate walk about the garden a bit? Henry, show Lucas the lake and the best fishing spots. We'll all take an hour or two to recover from the shock and then meet here again for tea. Difficult truths are always easier with tea."

Henry and Lucas bowed and left, and Catherine turned to go with Hannah. Lady Rampion hadn't moved or spoken, but her eyes never once left Catherine.

Outside again, she linked arms with Hannah and whispered,

CHAPTER 18

"Don't you think your mother ought to have said something to Lady Rampion? I thought she would faint. Perhaps she didn't want to see me again. What if I'm her natural child from a scandalous relationship?"

Hannah leaned her head so that it rested for a second against Catherine's. "She really ought to have been warned, I agree. But I don't think she was horrified or embarrassed to see you. Just startled. And… oh, I don't know. You'll think I'm silly. But it was like once she saw you, she couldn't get enough of seeing you, like she couldn't bear to look away."

"You think so?" That thought was much more warming than the fear that she was the cast off product of an illicit union.

"I do. But regardless, you'll get to find out the truth. That's what you wanted, isn't it?"

Catherine nodded.

Chapter 19

Lady Rampion's color was better by the time they returned to the drawing room. Tea was laid out on a low table. Henry and Lucas arrived just behind Hannah and Catherine, and Alice busied herself serving everyone. Catherine sat between Henry and Hannah, and she could feel Lady Rampion and Lucas both watching her. It struck her that she was sitting in a room with more people than she'd even known a week ago. She accepted her tea with a quiet "thank you," took a sip and a deep breath, and raised her gaze to theirs.

"I hope you'll excuse me." Lady Rampion's voice was soft and musical. "I'm staring, and I know it. I… I didn't know if I'd ever get to see you again. You've grown into a beautiful young woman."

Catherine blushed. "What happened?" she asked. "Why…?" She couldn't finish the question, but everyone knew what she meant.

Lady Rampion sighed. "We couldn't have children. For years and years. I was nineteen when I married Lord Rampion, and I watched all of my friends marry and start families. And every month my hopes sank. I felt like a failure. Rampion was unfailingly kind and affectionate; he never blamed me. But I knew he wanted a large family, and I let him down." She

CHAPTER 19

crumbled a tiny corner of cake between her fingers.

"One day I heard a rumor that if you went into a certain clearing on the night of a lunar eclipse and—oh, the instructions were silly, and I didn't know the first thing about magic.' She shook her head. "But they said that you could talk to a Faerie if you did it all just right, and by that point I was six-and-twenty and desperate. So I tried it—I snuck out of the house and into the woods. I followed the instructions exactly."

"Did you meet a Faerie?" Hannah breathed.

Lady Rampion's smile was tinged with regret. "I did. Not because I had done anything right, of course. I'd been told a load of rubbish. But someone else was in the same clearing at the same time, and *she* actually knew some magic. She had already summoned the Faerie and was making her own request."

"What was the Faerie like?" Hannah asked, on the edge of her seat, tea forgotten.

"Beautiful," Lady Rampion said. "Perfect in every respect. But... distant. More than just reserved." She paused and nibbled at the cake in her hand, taking a moment to process the memory. "Forgive me—I haven't spoken of that night in nearly twenty years. It's hard to describe it all"

"Take your time," the duchess said gently. "We have as long as you need."

Lady Rampion smiled at her before her eyes landed on Catherine again. "I had met Miss Anne Whitmer once or twice. She had a reputation for her skill with magic beyond the illusions most young ladies learned. I didn't hear what she had summoned the Faerie to request. To be honest, I didn't pause to listen. I threw myself at the Faerie's feet and pleaded for children. She listened calmly, then turned to Miss Whitmer.

Since Miss Whitmer had summoned her and offered her a bargain of some kind, the Faerie asked if she was moved to change the agreement.

"She looked at me for what felt like forever, and I didn't dare even breathe. Then she said she'd be willing to make a compromise. Miss Whitmer suggested that the Faerie give me four children, but that after the firstborn was weaned, I would give the babe to her to raise. She was a spinster, and her parents had recently died, and she was lonely. She would allow me to take part in her bargain with the Faerie under those conditions."

Lady Rampion's eyes glistened. "I took the deal. As I said, I was desperate, and even if I gave her one of my children, I'd have the other three. And she promised to take good care of the child and love it as her own. So, with her promise and the Faerie's, I left." She pressed her lips together, frowning down at her crumbled cake. "I conceived the next month, and I'd never felt such joy. And then I had you." She looked at Catherine, her eyes still swimming. "And I instantly regretted promising to give you away. You were so tiny and perfect. I couldn't tear my eyes from you. I wanted to watch every little thing you did because you were this beautiful miracle. But I only had one year with you before I had to uphold my end of the bargain. I hoped with all my heart that Miss Whitmer would change her mind, but on your first birthday, she arrived on our doorstep. She didn't say a word, just took you from my arms and left. And that was the last I heard of you."

She looked at Lucas. "Before long, I was increasing again, and Lucas was born, and then the twins, and we had three rambunctious boys under three years of age, and Rampion had the house full of children that he'd always wanted. But I

CHAPTER 19

secretly remembered your birthday every year."

The room fell silent as Lady Rampion took out a handkerchief and dabbed at her eyes. Catherine put her now cold tea on the table and sat back, trying to wrap her head around this whole story. Henry reached over and took her hand, and she grasped it gratefully, clinging to his warmth and solidity like an anchor.

Frowning, she said, "Mama—Miss Whitmer—wouldn't talk about where I'd come from, but she was afraid, so afraid, of losing me. I wondered, maybe, if there was a prophecy that something dreadful would happen to me."

"Not that I know of," Lady Rampion said. "Nothing dreadful to you, anyway." Catherine met her eyes, confused, and Lady Rampion blushed. "I might as well confess the rest. When I left the clearing that night, I—I hesitated. I heard Miss Whitmer and the Faerie… and I eavesdropped. The Faerie promised her the spells she'd asked for, but she warned Miss Whitmer that if she went through with this bargain, the girl-child would grow up to fall in love and marry, and Miss Whitmer would be left more alone than ever. I took it as good news—not for Miss Whitmer, of course, but for you, that you would know love." She smiled softly.

Catherine sank into her seat, deflated. Everything that Mama had done over the years had been to prevent her falling in love. It made sense now why Mama had reacted so strongly when Henry had kissed her. It hurt Catherine to know that she'd tried to keep her from knowing a husband's love. But it also made her sad. Mama had spent so many years lonely and afraid and desperate to keep Catherine all to herself.

"Everything she did trying to foil the prophecy," Catherine said softly, "only ended up fulfilling it."

"It's dangerous to listen to prophecies," Alice said wisely. "I've heard too many stories of people who have consorted with magicians or Fairies and learned that the hard way."

"You have?" Hannah asked. "Who?"

"Another time, dear," her mother said with a raised brow, just as the door opened and dinner was announced.

Dinner was oddly quiet. Catherine's mind swirled, and the others who had been in the room seemed similarly affected, though to a lesser degree. His Grace, Henry's father, observed the group, bemused. Mary was the only enthusiastic one at the table, and her focus was entirely on Lucas. She made no secret that she'd formed an instant attachment. To Catherine's surprise, Lucas seemed to relish the attention, perking up more than he had all afternoon.

In the drawing room after dinner, Lucas talked to Henry again, earnestly discussing fishing techniques, though his eyes were on Mary as often as not, and whenever he noticed her watching, which was often, his chest puffed up. Henry smothered his laughter, but his eyes glinted when he caught Catherine's, and she had to cover her mouth to hide her own smirk. Hannah hid her own amusement by pouring over music books at the pianoforte, taking longer than necessary to choose what to play. Alice and Lady Rampion had settled at a small table to one side, the duchess having provided their guest with writing supplies.

"Rampion was to stay another week in town before joining us at home, but under the circumstances…"

"You must send for him immediately," Alice said definitively. "Orson will have your letter sent express as soon as it is written."

Overhearing their conversation threw Catherine into confusion. It was enough of a shock to meet her mother, her

CHAPTER 19

actual mother who had given birth to her, and one younger brother. But she remembered abruptly that she also had a father, something she'd never known, and two other brothers. A pair of twins, no less. She suddenly had a whole family, and she didn't know what to think about it. They'd given her up when she was an infant, made a bargain before she was even born to surrender her. Her gaze fell on Lucas. Her brothers hadn't been alive then. She couldn't hold any of it against *them*. She watched as Lucas laughed at something Henry said. That smile was so *familiar*...

Catherine gasped. "Blackberries!"

Everyone turned to look at her. "Pardon?" Alice asked.

Catherine stared at her younger brother. "You're *Lucas*."

He glanced around the room to see if he was the only one confused. "Yes?" he said slowly. "Her Grace introduced us hours ago, didn't she?"

Catherine shook her head. "No. Yes, she did, but no, I meant you're the boy I picked blackberries with. Years ago, when your carriage needed repairs and you snuck away into the woods."

Comprehension dawned on half of their faces. "You're *that* Lucas," Henry said.

"You mean to say that *this* was the Catherine you told us about? I thought you made her up." Lady Rampion's eyes widened.

"I told you I didn't!" exclaimed Lucas. "You punished me extra for lying."

"I hope you didn't get into too much trouble," Catherine frowned. "You told me your twin brothers would keep them so distracted they'd never notice you were gone."

Lucas rubbed the back of his neck, chagrinned. "Oh, they noticed. I got in a boatload of trouble, first because I'd run off and then because I got sick from all the blackberries I'd eaten."

Catherine laughed. She'd liked Lucas as a child, and she liked him now. He was exactly what she'd imagined a brother would be.

***

The next day life settled back into something of the normal routine for Cauldercrest. Catherine and Hannah walked out with art supplies, and Hannah laughed at Catherine's delight at drawing a new scene she hadn't sketched or painted a hundred times over. At dinner, Lady Rampion made a quiet but distinct effort to get to know Catherine, talking about music and drawing and all the things young ladies were usually interested in. Catherine wanted to like her, but she kept her distance; she wasn't sure she was ready to forgive the woman for giving her away so willingly.

Lucas, on the other hand, continued to win her over by regaling her—and Henry and Mary, who were sitting nearby in the drawing room—with stories of mishaps he and the twins had gotten into when they were younger, and some of what the twins still got into. They were fourteen now, but according to Lucas they hadn't matured one iota in the last six years.

Henry took Catherine out for a walk the next morning before breakfast. They wandered the gardens slowly, hand in hand. The longer it was just the two of them alone, the more the weight of the past few days lifted from Catherine. She sighed and wondered aloud, "Do you think Mama forbid me from seeing anyone because Lucas was a boy or because she knew he was my brother?" It was one of the many questions that had plagued her, keeping sleep at bay for hours each night.

CHAPTER 19

Henry considered. "Most likely because he was a boy," he said finally, "though it's not hard to tell you're siblings. Maybe she didn't know, but the idea that he *could* be your brother frightened her. It reminded her of the deal she'd made and the secrets she kept."

Catherine nodded. After another moment of silence, she said, "I like Lucas. I think I'll enjoy having a brother."

"It's what you've always wanted." Henry squeezed her hand. "What of Lady Rampion? What do you think of her?"

"I don't know," she said softly. "She chose not to keep me before I was even born. Like I was disposable."

They reached the shadow of an old oak whose trunk and canopy blocked them from view of the house. Henry pulled her close and held her. She rested her head against his shoulder and breathed in his comforting scent of soap and mint and something all Henry. He rested his cheek against her head.

"I confess," he murmured, "I'm rather glad she made that bargain. If she hadn't, you might not exist. And your existence is of the utmost importance to me."

Catherine smiled slightly. She hadn't thought about it that way. Without the deal with the Faerie, she and her brothers may never have been born. If Lady Rampion hadn't given her to Mama, she wouldn't have been in the garden singing when Henry happened by and heard her. Perhaps they would have met some other way, but no one could ever really know what might have been. What they had between them was too precious to wish for things to be different.

A voice shook them from the moment.

"I say, you're getting a bit cozy with my sister," Lucas accused, frozen in the act of coming around a corner.

Catherine bit back a smile. She regretted the interruption,

but she'd wondered what it would be like to have a protective brother, and she couldn't help finding it amusing. "Lucas, we're engaged," she said, stepping a little away from Henry, but letting her hand find his again.

Her brother looked between the two of them, a grin spreading across his face. "Engaged? Blimey, that's something. Still, though, none of this…" He waved his hand awkwardly toward them in place of words he didn't want to speak.

Catherine did laugh then, and even Henry chuckled, and the two of them fell in with Lucas as they all returned to the house.

Chapter 20

Lord Rampion arrived late that afternoon. Henry and his father greeted him in the entrance hall before Orson took him to freshen up for dinner. Rampion was taller than Lucas, with receding silver hair and clear, pale gray eyes. He had probably been lanky like his son when he was younger, but he'd thickened about the middle since then.

"Is it true?" Rampion asked, shaking first Father's hand then Henry's. "Milly wrote that our daughter is here—is it true?"

"Quite so," Father said with a smile. "Kate's a delightful girl and a good friend of Hannah's."

Rampion blanched slightly, and he spoke in a choked whisper. "Milly used to call her Kate."

Henry blinked. Had Catherine known, somehow, in the recesses of her memory, that she'd always been Kate?

He was still wondering about it when dinner was announced. Before they were seated, Rampion was introduced to Kate, and Henry saw her shy for almost the first time. She answered when spoken to, but she was quiet, and she avoided everyone's eyes. Which meant that she spent most of dinner looking at her plate, because her father, like her mother two days ago, couldn't look away from her.

Henry pulled her aside in the drawing room afterwards. "Are

you all right?"

She nodded. He thought she looked pale, but she smiled ruefully. "I've never had a father before. It's a lot to take in."

Henry wanted to hold her, kiss her, comfort her, but both of their families surrounded them. He settled for squeezing her hand.

Lady Rampion crossed the room to join them, with her husband at her heels. "Kate," she said hesitantly, "I know I've long since forfeited any parental rights, and I can't apologize enough. But we're family, and we want you to know... we'd be honored if you'd be Catherine Templeton again." She glanced at her husband and her cheeks flamed. "We understand if you want to keep the name of your adopted mother, but..." She shook her head weakly.

Hannah, overhearing, stepped closer. "Miss Templeton does have a nice ring to it." She winked at Kate, knowing as well as Henry did how much she hated to be called Miss Whitmer.

Kate froze like a startled deer. Henry leaned closer to say softly, "You don't have to decide now, you know. And no matter which name you choose, I'll call you Kate." She looked up at him, and he saw her tension thaw slightly. "Besides, it won't be long before you exchange it for Stanton."

A slow smile spread over her face. Suddenly her eyes widened, as if she'd been hit by an epiphany. "I have parents," she whispered.

"You do." Henry couldn't stop his own smile from growing. "Shall I ask them?"

Kate nodded.

"Ask us what?" demanded Rampion.

Henry turned to him, taking Kate's hand and tucking it through his arm. "Kate has agreed to marry me," he said, flashing a quick smile at her. "Miss Whitmer opposed the match. We were anticipating a trip to Scotland, but Kate deserves a proper wedding surrounded by family... if you'll give your consent?"

Lady Rampion's eyes filled with tears, and she wordlessly embraced them both. Her husband blustered but gave his hearty consent to the match, declaring that he couldn't think of a finer fellow. As the rest of the family joined the celebration, Henry murmured in Kate's ear, "It might be less confusing for the rector if you shared your parents' surname."

She nodded. "It was just so sudden. I think I'd prefer Templeton anyway. For a short while, at least." Her shy smile left him in no doubt of her meaning, and if it weren't for everyone else in the room, he'd have had her in his arms in a heartbeat.

***

"The modiste will be arriving from town this morning," Alice said at breakfast a few days later, raising her cup of chocolate to her lips. "Madame Evangeline will take your measurements and get started on your dress right away."

"Oh, but I was going to—" Catherine protested, looking up from her own tea and realizing that she'd been about to argue with a duchess.

Only a few members of the two families were at the table, but they all looked at her.

"What, Kate?" Henry asked when she didn't finish. "What were you going to do? I'm sure the modiste can wait a few hours for whatever it is."

Catherine dropped her gaze to her plate and said quietly, "I was hoping to borrow a carriage or a horse to go to the tower."

A chorus of alarmed cries greeted this.

"Only to get some of my things," she explained quickly. "And... I guess I'd like to reconcile with Mama. I'll never go back to live with her, but we parted on such very bad terms."

She met Henry's eyes. A mix of sympathy and concern shone from them. He was the only other person who knew exactly how unfriendly their parting had been.

"I can't let you go alone," he said gently. "I'll come with you. Perhaps Father should come as well—everyone listens to a duke."

"I'll come along as well," Lord Rampion said. Catherine still couldn't call him father, even in her head. The concept was too foreign. But she was slowly getting used to the idea. "I may not have the clout of His Grace, but I'm Kate's father, and I'd like to see where she was raised."

So after breakfast, the four of them climbed into the landau. The driver stopped on the road and stayed with the horses as they disembarked and followed the path through the woods on foot. Catherine felt like she was barely breathing, between her nerves about facing Mama and having the three gentlemen following behind her. What would their fathers think of the tower? What might Mama do to them all, if she hadn't returned to her former rational self?

What she saw when she emerged at the edge of the garden put all those worries from her mind. The garden was overgrown, rampant with weeds as if it had been neglected for years rather than weeks. The tower itself was crumbling, chunks of rock missing from the walls that had stood firm for her entire life. Small plants grew in the cracks between weathered, lichen-covered stones. Gone was the well-maintained home she

CHAPTER 20

remembered. It was a ruin.

Catherine stopped, staring, her mouth agape, then she ran forward.

"Kate!" Henry called after her.

She didn't slow, and she could hear his footsteps pounding on the flagstones behind her. She darted around previously neat flower beds and jumped over the birdbath, lying on its side in two broken pieces. Henry caught up to her as she reached the door. The massive stones from the wall that had fallen in the autumn storm had fallen farther and settled so that there was a gap just wide enough for a person to fit through. The wooden door was so rotten that it fell to pieces when she pulled on the handle. With a cry, Catherine shoved her way into the kitchen. But it wasn't a kitchen any longer. It was just a round, empty chamber in a ruined tower, with no sign that anyone had lived there.

Henry caught her arm, keeping her from attempting to rush up the stairs. He pulled her close. "It's not safe, sweetheart," he said, stroking her back, her hair.

Catherine buried her face in his shoulder and sobbed. "I didn't think she *meant* it!" Mama had kept her word to never see Catherine again, had left, had vanished without giving her a chance to reconcile. The magic maintaining the tower was gone, thoroughly erasing Catherine's entire childhood. She had nothing to show for the last nineteen years of her life—no family, no home, no belongings. Cut adrift, she clung to Henry until the tears subsided.

Once she was only sniffling weakly, Henry let go just long enough to dig out a handkerchief for her. She wiped her face and blew her nose, then he took her by the hand and led her gently from the tower. Outside in the garden, she took a deep breath, the scents familiar and comforting despite the garden's unkempt state.

"I'm taking Kate for a short walk," Henry told their fathers, who were examining the tower and ruined walls. "We'll meet you back at the carriage."

Neither lord argued, casting only the briefest glances at Catherine's tear-stained face before nodding. She allowed Henry to lead her out of the garden and into the woods on the far side, not caring where they were going. The babble of the stream was the first thing to break through the numbness. They stepped into the clearing, and it all washed over her: the moss underfoot, the dappled tree shadows, the chattering water, the smell of damp earth and growing things. She stood and let it fill her up, and Henry came around to stand behind her, sliding his arms around her waist and resting his cheek against her head. They were silent for a long time, just being there together. Catherine knew without asking why Henry had brought her. He knew she'd lost everything, and he was reminding her that this was still here. This place, with all of its memories, still existed unchanged. *All* of her memories still existed, even if Mama and the tower were gone.

At last, Catherine turned in Henry's arms, wrapping her own around his neck, and kissed him. "Thank you," she whispered.

"I love you." He kissed her temple. "Our fathers are waiting, and our mothers are probably impatient to start with your dress fitting."

Catherine nodded and stepped back. "I'll need a whole new wardrobe now." She glanced down at the borrowed pomona green gown she'd borrowed from Hannah.

"Good thing the modiste is coming." Henry took her hand, and together they started back along the path.

CHAPTER 20

***

Catherine was hiding in the garden when Henry found her a few days later. She'd discovered that few people spent any time in the maze, and once she'd memorized the turns, she could spend a quiet half hour alone before anyone called for her. Henry didn't bother calling; he also knew the route through the maze and found her sitting on a shaded bench.

She smiled up at him, chagrinned, but he didn't remark on her interesting choice of location. He sat beside her, and after a moment, said, "Everyone keeps asking where I'm taking you on our honeymoon." His hand found hers. Catherine was dumbstruck by his incredible smile and the sincerity in his eyes. "I want to take you everywhere, show you everything. But what do *you* want to see? What would make you happy, Kate?"

Catherine gaped at him. He was too impossibly good and caring. "Would you be upset," she hesitated, "if I told you I didn't want to see *any*thing just yet?" She bit her lip. "I didn't realize that having a family would mean never having a moment's privacy. There's always someone talking to me. I've been through a whole wardrobe of fittings, and now they're talking about adding another gown because they want to hold a ball for us in a month or two."

"You've wanted to attend a ball," Henry reminded her.

"I have. I do. But right now all I want is to go someplace where you and I can be together, just the two of us, with no one else."

Rather than being disappointed that she didn't want to embark on a Grand Tour, Henry's slow smile lit up. "I know just the thing," he said. "Meet me out front in a quarter hour."

He kissed her cheek and hurried from the maze.

Mystified, Catherine rose and followed slowly after. By the time she walked down the front steps, a phaeton was pulling around. Henry exited the house behind her and lifted her into the seat, taking the reins from the groom.

"Where are we going?" Catherine asked.

"You'll see." Henry grinned. "We could have walked, but it's a beautiful day for a drive, and the modiste is asking for you. I promised we wouldn't be long."

He drove them down the drive toward the main gate, but before they reached it, he turned off onto a side path. It wound around a copse of trees before revealing a lovely little cottage, nestled in its own garden with trees for shade and privacy. Henry jumped down and helped Catherine, then led her to the front door. He pulled a key from his pocket and unlocked it, leaving it open wide behind them so that the sunlight shone on the gleaming wood floors.

"My grandmother lived in this dower house for years after my father inherited. It's been empty since she died, but it's in good condition. Just needs a little freshening up." He looked around and then back at Catherine. "What do you think?"

Catherine was used to rooms having corners by now, but these rooms were much smaller than the ones in the main house. They were cozy, and though most of the furniture was covered in sheets, a peek underneath told her the furnishings would be comfortable and elegant without being fussy. Multiple windows let in plenty of sunlight. Catherine wandered from room to room, opening every door before looking up at Henry.

"It's perfect."

He beamed. "Good. Because I've asked Father, and it's ours

CHAPTER 20

for as long as we want it."

"You mean it? We get to live here—alone?"

Henry laughed. "With a handful of servants, but yes. They'll have it ready for us to live here in time for the wedding. I was thinking they could hang the watercolor you gave me in the bedroom—I had it framed, you know."

Catherine's heart felt fit to burst. "Thank you." She went up on tiptoes to kiss Henry's cheek. "You're giving me everything I've ever wanted." Her eyes searched his. "But what about you? It's not fair for me to be the only one whose dreams are coming true."

"The only one?" Henry shook his head, and gold bubbled up within the muddy hazel of his eyes. "I'm about to spend the rest of my life with the most beautiful, genuine woman I've ever met. I get to wake up beside you every morning and kiss you whenever I like." He bent down to brush his lips lightly against hers. "I've wanted to give you the world from the very beginning." He reached into his pocket. "And I wanted to give you *this* ages ago."

He slipped a band of braided brown leather over her wrist. A small piece tooled in a pattern that reminded her of lilacs joined the band into a circle.

"You made this for me?"

"Hannah wouldn't let me give it to you for Christmas for fear it would cause trouble with your mother."

"I love it."

"I did *not* make this."

He produced a ring from his pocket, delicate and golden, with a small diamond surrounded by sapphires. He took Catherine's left hand and slid the ring onto her finger. "*You* are my dream come true, Kate."

She was speechless. Henry took the opportunity to kiss her again, and she melted in his arms. When they broke apart, Henry said, "We should get you back for that fitting," but he made no move to leave.

"We should," Catherine agreed, content to stand there with him for hours.

Eventually, they meandered back out of the house. Henry pointed to a corner of the sitting room as they passed and suggested that the new harp he'd ordered from town would fit nicely there.

"Will you sing for me sometimes?" he asked once they were back in the phaeton.

"I'll sing for you as often as you like," Catherine said, sliding closer and leaning her head on his shoulder. "I'll even make up ridiculous songs about May to remind you of the first time we met."

"I would have fallen in love with you no matter what you'd been singing," he said, laughing. "You stole my heart that day and never let go."

She hummed a sigh, smiling. "And I never intend to."

***

Thank you for reading Kate and Henry's story! I hope you enjoyed it as much as I did. If you loved it, please leave a review on Goodreads or your favorite retailer to help another reader find a book they'll love.

It means so much to me that you've taken the time to experience my alternate Regency England. If you want to learn more and be the first to know about upcoming books, cover reveals, freebies, and other goodies, join my newsletter at elizaprokopovits.com/newsletter.

CHAPTER 20

And read on for the first chapter of the next book in the Regency Magic Faerie Tales, Her Accidental Frog, *a retelling of "The Frog Prince"—Hannah and Johnson's story!*

Happy reading!
Eliza

CHAPTER 20

Her Accidental Frog: Chapter 1

Nathaniel Johnson was having inarguably the worst morning of his life.

He'd been expecting a hangover, but this? He'd come to only a half hour ago, and it had taken this whole time to make sense of his predicament. If only he could remember more of what happened last night.

He remembered going out with Wortle to the public house and drinking a shocking amount of ale and blue ruin. Nathaniel made a mental note—reiterating the one he'd made last night—that Wortle might not be the best companion of an evening if he didn't want to end up foxed. After midnight, the memories grew vague, but there had been a bit of an altercation with some fellow in a dark coat. The man had called him out, though Nathaniel couldn't for the life of him remember why. They'd decided to settle their dispute immediately, forgoing seconds. They'd taken a hack to Nathaniel's lodgings for his dueling pistols and then made their drunken way to Hyde Park, which was quiet as death at two in the morning. They'd found an out-of-the-way spot, paced out the distance, and...

And then everything had gone dark. Darker, that is, than the middle of the night in Hyde Park. Nathaniel couldn't remember a thing after that until a half hour ago, when he woke up without an injury, without a headache, without his pistols, and without a clue how he'd ended up in the Serpentine.

As a frog.

It had taken several minutes of splashing and thrashing before he figured it out. But then it couldn't be ignored: the webbed feet, the slick skin, the desperate croaks coming from his own throat. The fact that the reeds along the bank looked so very much taller than he would have expected.

Must have been a bloody magician, he thought grimly. *Dirty cheat. The chosen weapon was pistols, not magic.*

Nathaniel would gladly have settled the score, but he was hardly in a position to do so, besides having no idea of the fellow's name. Served him right for getting into a duel while in his cups. Another mental note: no more blue ruin. Ever.

Then again—no. It didn't serve him right. The man was a cad. Nathaniel wallowed for a few minutes in the unfairness of it all, before shaking himself out of it and looking forward. What was he to do? How was he to break this blasted curse and become human again? Aside from the obvious reasons remaining an amphibian wouldn't do, he had a commitment to attend his father in Devon at the start of June, and too much rode on it to miss. He had two months, but in his helpless state, he was unlikely to solve his problem in two years, let alone a shorter time. His only hope was another magician, but how was he to find one in his current situation?

A voice on the shore froze his froggy blood to ice. "I'll only look for a minute, and then I'll come back." Nathaniel knew that musical voice. His ear had become attuned to it, listening for it at every assembly. It belonged to the person he usually hoped most to see, now the one person he wished to avoid. Lady Hannah Stanton.

***

Lady Hannah Stanton had high hopes for this Season. Not only were her brother Henry and his new wife Kate in town, but her younger sister Mary had prevailed upon their mother to allow her to come out early at just barely seventeen. Hannah was less surprised by this concession than she might have been, though she herself had entered Society at nearly nineteen. Mary was the baby of the family; when she wanted something, she generally got it. With Mama's attention on launching Mary into Society properly, Hannah could enjoy her third Season in London without being subjected to her mother's heavy-handed matchmaking.

Of course, a younger sister's debut also meant hosting a ball for her at the house in Berkeley Square, or at least it did when their parents were the Duke and Duchess of Caulder, even though Mary had already attended half a dozen assemblies and soirees since they arrived in town.

And a ball meant new gowns and fittings and rather a lot of hubbub.

Not that Hannah minded. She loved balls, and she loved Mary and her sister-in-law Kate, who was nineteen, a year younger than Hannah. Kate had grown up extremely sheltered and, until they arrived in town nearly two months ago, had never experienced a true London crush, where the assembly was packed so tightly that one could hardly dance. Mary's experience of balls had been equally limited. Hannah had been looking forward all year to showing her new friend around town while her mother managed Mary's introduction.

This morning, however, had been spent at home in a final fitting for their ballgowns, as Mary's coming-out ball was only three days away. Hannah had stood on a stool in her mother's lavish dressing room while Madame Evangeline, her mother's preferred French modiste, tutted and made a few final adjustments. Sunlight had streamed through the glazed windows, and she'd been so afraid that clouds would take over before she could get outside. At last, they were finished, and Hannah and Mary together rushed out the door, tying on bonnets and tugging on gloves as they went.

Hannah tipped her head back, slowing her stride and letting the sun warm her face.

"That defeats the purpose of wearing a bonnet, you know," Mary teased. "You might as well leave it off."

"If we were at home, I would," Hannah agreed. "But it wouldn't do to shock the *ton* right before your ball."

"But you don't mind if you freckle before the ball?"

Hannah made a face at her sister. They both had the same problem—a little kiss from the sun and their noses and cheeks sported a dusting of freckles. This rarely stopped Hannah from going without a bonnet, but she had high popes for this ball....
She tipped her head back down so that her face was shaded.

"Now that you've ruined your complexion, could you walk a little faster? I'd like to reach the park before everyone else leaves it."

Hannah picked up her pace. It was a longish walk to Hyde Park, but she loved the wide open green and the curving Serpentine. Mary enjoyed watching the people—on most fine mornings, everyone who was anyone could be seen driving or walking through the park, so that half the time traffic was at a standstill. Hannah preferred the flowers and little glimpse of nature she could get in the middle of London.

Mary needn't have feared. Members of the *beau monde* still crowded the lanes, greeting each other from horseback or from phaetons or curricles. It would only get busier as the

Season progressed and the weather grew pleasanter. The two girls were stopped several times by acquaintances, their pace slowing to a meander. Near the bank of the Serpentine, they fell in with a pair of Mary's particular friends, the Miss Lemmons, Elise and Christine. Hannah allowed her attention to drift as the younger girls chatted excitedly about the prospect of the ball and the other entertainments of the coming week. She noticed several flower beds with tiny green shoots and promised herself to come back in a few days to see their progress. Her gaze settled on the Serpentine, whose still water reflected the rarest of blue skies. Movement near the bank caught her eye, and she took a step toward it without thinking.

"What is it, Hannah?" Mary asked, breaking off from her description of the hothouse flowers Mama had ordered.

"I saw something in the water," Hannah answered, never taking her eyes from where she'd seen the motion. "It might have been a frog, though it's a bit early for them."

Miss Lemmon made a sound of disgust, while Miss Christine let out a little shriek. "*Frogs?* Really?" They edged away from the water, though they were nowhere near the bank where they stood.

"Please leave it, Hannah," Mary pleaded in a whisper. "I don't want to go look at frogs or fish or grasshoppers or… anything that could jump at me."

Hannah bit her lip. When they were children, she used to explore the lake on their estate at Cauldercrest with their older brothers, Henry and Daniel, tagging along regardless of whether the boys wanted her to. Once they'd gone off to school, however, she'd had no one to share her discoveries with, and she'd dragged Mary along on more than one occasion.

"You stay and talk with your friends," she said. "Just keep

within sight. I'll only look for a minute, and then I'll come back."

Mary let out a long-suffering sigh but returned to her conversation. Hannah grinned and crossed to the reedy bank. She shot one more glance back at her sister, who was arm in arm with Miss Lemmon and walking slowly. It suddenly struck her as funny how people could be so alike and so different simultaneously. Mary shared the same brown hair, hazel eyes, and sun-induced freckles as Hannah, though Hannah's face was rounder. Mary was only an inch or so taller than Hannah, but she shared the same propensity toward curves rather than the straight, willowy figures of the Lemmon sisters. Both of them loved dancing and music, and both had determination in spades.

And yet, Hannah was certain that Mary would fit into Society much better than she did. Mary was so bubbly and energetic, a natural flirt and gossip, which would endear her to half the *ton*. Hannah had never once been called reserved, but compared to her sister, she felt it. And then there was her inconvenient interest in wildlife…

She turned her attention back to the water and crouched down, holding still and breathing softly as her brothers had showed her so that she wouldn't disturb whatever creatures were there.

***

Nathaniel looked to the bank and saw Hannah crouching down. Her bonnet hid her eyes, but he could see her pretty pink mouth curved in a small smile as she went still and silent. He'd always found that amazing about her, how she overflowed with life one moment and then tamped it all down to become part of the scenery the next. He swam closer, unable to help himself. The movement caught her eye, and he froze under her gaze.

Breathe, he told himself. *She doesn't know who you are. She doesn't know that you've proven yourself to be the biggest fool in London.*

They stared at each other for another moment before she glanced over her shoulder at a cluster of young ladies. Mary must be waiting for her. Hannah sat back on her heels. As she made a move to go, Nathaniel panicked. However he felt about Hannah, he couldn't let this chance pass him by.

"Help," he croaked, swimming closer. "Help."

She froze, staring. "That's not the sound they usually make," she muttered to herself.

Nathaniel hopped onto the bank, stopping several feet from her and holding her gaze. "Help. Please."

"Good heavens," she breathed. "Who are you?"

He'd much rather not admit that.

"Human," he croaked.

She blinked. "Oh dear. *Which* human? What's your name?"

Nathaniel cringed, but there was nothing for it. Confessing his stupidity to the most wonderful girl in England was a fair penance for his foolhardiness last night—and another reminder never to drink, if this was the humiliation that followed. But when he opened his mouth, nothing happened. He couldn't croak a single sound, let alone a word. His name lodged like a rock in his throat. What was happening? He gulped, blinked, and tried again.

Still nothing.

"Do you not remember? Or can you not say?"

Nathaniel was trying, but his name, his father's title, anything that would reveal his identity to Hannah—it was all locked inside him with no way out. He finally tried to say something different. "Help," he repeated weakly.

He sounded pathetic, but at least he got the word out.

"Of course I'll help," Hannah said, reaching slowly toward him and resting her open, gloved hands on the ground for him to hop into. "I'll take you to Kate. She's a magician, and she's got a spell that can pause or undo other spells—I'm not sure how it works exactly, but I've seen her use it." Her hands were warm under Nathaniel's feet, and the kid leather was soft. She slowly raised him up to eye level. "We'll get you sorted right away. Do you mind riding in my pocket for now? Mary's a bit squeamish about things that jump."

She shifted him over to one hand and with the other held open the pocket of her skirt. Then she lowered him slowly into it, and he hopped from her hand and settled against the fabric. The walking dress was dark green and blocked out the light. When Hannah rose to her feet, the swooping motion of her skirt made Nathaniel momentarily dizzy. Coupled with the heady scent of her lightly floral perfume, he felt almost as untethered as he'd been last night under the gin's influence.

A light pressure as she gently put her hand against the outside of the pocket. "Are you all right in there?"

"Good," he croaked.

They both fell silent, which was a relief. Frogs weren't designed for talking, so forcing out a syllable or two with each croak was hard work. He wouldn't have minded listening to Hannah talk, but when she joined her sister and they'd said goodbye to their friends, Mary was the one whose chatter filled the air. Nathaniel let his mind wander. Mary's conversation had always been filled with parties and gossip, though when he'd first been introduced to the Stantons of Cauldercrest, her parties had been imaginary fêtes held by her dolls. The rhythm of Hannah's walk was slow and soothing, and it lulled him into a state of calm he hadn't thought within his reach.

He could feel when Hannah climbed the steps to the front door and the change in the air when they crossed the threshold. A pause and a rustle, as bonnets and gloves were removed, then a few more steps before Hannah hesitated.

"Have you seen Kate?" she asked.

Nathaniel could hear her mother's voice, muffled slightly by the pocket. "Henry took her to a museum once her fitting was over. I'm not sure which one. Something wrong, dear?"

"No, not at all. Just something I wanted to ask her." The lightness in her voice sounded forced, but only slightly.

More movement, more stairs, and then the closing of a door. A quiet splashing sound that made Nathaniel's skin ache with thirst. Was that possible? Apparently for a frog. Hannah's bare hand slipped into the pocket. Her skin was distractingly soft as she scooped him up and lifted him out. Daylight from the window made him blink a few times before he realized that she was lowering him gently into a washbasin filled halfway with water from the nearby pitcher. It wasn't as cold as the Serpentine, but it was cool and deliciously wet. He splashed and cavorted and delighted in the feeling before settling with his eyes just above the surface. Hannah was laughing, and Nathaniel found he didn't mind that she was laughing at him, because the sound made his heart dance.

"Feel better?" She grinned. She sat on the edge of the bed, and Nathaniel suddenly realized that he was in her bedchamber. His heart pounded even faster at that. He'd never once seen the inside of this room, nor had he ever intended to. But

Hannah was talking again, so he dragged his thoughts back. "We'll have to talk to Kate after dinner. In the meantime, you can stay here rather than suffering in my pocket. Here." She grabbed a small decorative pillow from the bed, the linen cover embroidered with lilies. She set it on the washstand beside the bowl. "Something comfortable if you want to be out of the water. Please stay on this table where you're safe, Mr. Frog."

A groan came out as a strangled croak.

"I know," she said, her brow furrowing. "It's a terrible name, isn't it? But I must have something to call you. You truly can't tell me your real name?"

Nathaniel tried to say his name again, but it lodged in his throat like before. All he could do was blink at her.

"Very well, then, I'll have to come up with something." She studied him. "You're a common frog, *Rana temporaria*, so... I'll call you... Tempo?"

He'd forgotten her impressive memory for scientific names. Hearing her say the Latin name now took him back to the very first time he'd stayed at Cauldercrest when he was fourteen. His father, the Earl of Bembry, had taken his mother on the Grand Tour of Europe. His mother had been lifelong friends with the Duchess of Caulder, and as he and Henry were the same age, he'd been invited to stay with them for the summer rather than being stuck alone at home with his tutor. That summer, in addition to being the start of his lifelong friendship with Henry, was one of the best of his life, full of racing around the estate with Henry and his brother Daniel, climbing trees, riding horses, playing cricket. They'd spent hours searching for tadpoles and minnows in the shallows of the lake. Hannah had left Mary to her dolls and followed the boys around as often as she could. He could still picture her, nine years old, barefoot with her skirt tucked up into the waistband, up to her knees in the water, and telling anyone who'd listen about the types of frogs they might find and what their proper Latin names were. Her brothers had rolled their eyes and humored her, muttering to him that she'd stumbled across some natural history texts in the library and wouldn't shut up about it now.

Hannah raised an eyebrow at him, and he realized she was waiting for a response. "Will that do?"

"Naturalist." It took two croaks to get the word out.

She smiled. "A very amateur one, I suppose. I've always found creatures and plants fascinating." She tilted her head to the side. "So Tempo will do?"

Nathaniel nodded. It was better than Mr. Frog.

"Good. And let's pray that your condition really is *temporaria*." She smiled at the wordplay. "Now, Kate will probably need to know how you ended up this way. Can you tell me what happened?"

If Nathaniel's green skin could have flushed, it would have been beet red. "Duel," he muttered. "Magician." If he could have turned redder, he would have. If there were anywhere to hide in the basin, he would have done that, too. But he had to admit the truth. "Trifle. Foxed."

Hannah's mouth fell open. "You got into a drunken duel with a magician? Good heavens."

He blinked, chagrin and mortification practically oozing from him. "He used. Magic. Not. Pistol."

Her eyes widened. "That's not sporting. Do you know what spell he used?"

Nathaniel shook his head.

"Hmm. Well, hopefully this is enough for Kate to go on. I have to dress for dinner now, but I'll be back to collect you."

She disappeared through the doorway into the dressing room, and Nathaniel sank below the water with a sigh. He hadn't wrestled with such a confusing mix of emotions in years, if ever. Hannah alone raised feelings of elation, humiliation, dread, and joy, and that wasn't touching on the hope and fear that gripped him as he thought of Henry's wife's spells or his helpless fury at the unknown magician. A frog was far too small to contain so much. He swam restless laps in the basin in a vain attempt to control it all.

Also by Eliza Prokopovits

Ember and Twine

Jewels and Dragons

The Thunderstone Theft

Regency Magic Faerie Tales
   Her Fae Secret
   The Beast's Magician
   Her Forgotten Sea
   Her Cursed Apple
   Her Enchanted Tower
   Her Accidental Frog

About the Author

Eliza Prokopovits (pro-COP-o-vits) is a writer and knitting designer. She is obsessed with books, yarn, and dark chocolate. She lives in Pennsylvania with her husband, two boys, and aging goldendoodle.

www.ingramcontent.com/pod-product-compliance
Ingram Content Group UK Ltd.
Pitfield, Milton Keynes, MK11 3LW, UK
UKHW022210230426
12048UKWH00016BA/752